THE DANGERS
OF DATING
YOUR BOSS

BY
SUE MacKAY

First published in Great Britain 2012
by Mills & Boon, an imprint of Harlequin (UK) Limited.
Large Print edition 2012
Harlequin (UK) Limited, Eton House,
18-24 Paradise Road, Richmond, Surrey TW9 1SR

© Sue MacKay 2012

ISBN: 978 0 263 22486 3

Harlequin (UK) policy is to use papers that are natural, renewable and recyclable products and made from wood grown in sustainable forests. The logging and manufacturing process conform to the legal environmental regulations of the country of origin.

Printed and bound in Great Britain
by CPI Antony Rowe, Chippenham, Wiltshire

With a background of working in medical laboratories and a love of the romance genre, it is no surprise that **Sue MacKay** writes Medical Romance stories. An avid reader all her life, she wrote her first story at age eight—about a prince, of course. She lives with her own hero in the beautiful Marlborough Sounds, at the top of New Zealand's South Island, where she indulges her passions for the outdoors, the sea and cycling.

Also by Sue MacKay:

SURGEON IN A WEDDING DRESS
RETURN OF THE MAVERICK
PLAYBOY DOCTOR TO DOTING DAD
THEIR MARRIAGE MIRACLE

These books are also available in eBook format from www.millsandboon.co.uk

Behind every author is a great editor.
Thank you, Megan Haslam,
for your patience and wonderful encouragement.

CHAPTER ONE

'IF I DON'T eat in the next five minutes I'm going to slip into a coma,' Ruby Smith told her boss and crew partner, Dave.

'Yeah, yeah. Heard it all before. Didn't you have breakfast?' Dave stacked the two medical packs at the helicopter door, ready to be taken into the storeroom and replenished.

'That was hours ago.' She glanced at her watch. 'Six hours ago, to be precise.' A call had come through as she'd been about to sit down to a hot steak pie from the local bakery. Now they'd just returned from an MVA on State Highway One. They'd airlifted a young man with both femurs broken and one femoral artery torn to Hutt Hospital.

'Hey, Red, is that you?' A deep, male voice with a slight rasp called from down on the tarmac.

Ruby's heart leapt into her throat. Jack? Even

after years apart, that voice was as familiar to her as her own. And it still had the power to unravel her carefully put-together resolve to keep him at arm's length. That voice had been what had first attracted her to Jack, the only man she'd ever loved. The man she'd walked away from. For the dumbest of reasons.

But what was Jack doing here? Today? He wasn't due to start until Monday, when she'd have been prepared. Right now she was still getting her head around all the ramifications of working with him. Would it be like old times? Jack the consummate professional watching her like a hawk, always teaching her, helping her improve her nursing skills? And would she be listening impatiently, wanting to touch him every time no one was looking? A sigh tickled over her lip. Want to or not, she had to keep her hands to herself. She'd go around with them jammed in her pockets if necessary. She'd moved on, grown up, knew her worth. So if there were a few blips between them as they got used to working together again, she'd survive.

There was no choice. Wellington was home now. Never again would she toss her few possessions into her pack and head away. She'd even burnt that pack against the day wanderlust struck again. She'd done her searching, found what she'd been looking for and sucked up the pain from knowing she'd wasted years of her life because of it. To let Jack back under her skin would risk her newfound and fragile contentment.

She peered out into the glittering winter sun, gripping the doorframe, her knuckles white. Jack, tall and slim, emanated strength in his stance as he stared up at her. Her mouth dried. Solid need sliced through her, heating and freezing her all at once. Need she believed she'd finally wrestled into submission. Jack Forbes. Her new boss and crew partner. Her old lover.

She couldn't do this. She had to do this. 'Hi, Jack,' she managed feebly. *Hi, gorgeous,* her brain mocked her.

He grinned his well-practised, impish grin that had always got him everything he wanted, including her. 'Get your butt out of that flying machine and come say hello to an old mate.'

So that was how he was going to play it. Mates. She could work with that, and it was a better start than she'd hoped for. Ruby jumped down onto the tarmac, grimacing as she jarred her bung knee. Tugging her shoulders back tight, she strode towards the moment she'd been both looking forward to and dreading since returning home to New Zealand. She strode towards Jack, apparently her friend. She hadn't been sure if she was as over this man as she should be. And now? The jury was out.

'Jack, it's great to see you.' Talk about the understatement of the year. Of her life.

'Great to see ya, ruby-red girl.' His old greeting. The one he'd shouted out as he'd come in the door at night, when he'd rolled over in bed in the morning.

Ruby's heart tripped. Ruby-red girl. Did he even realise what he'd said? She blinked up at him, saw his Adam's apple bob and shoved down the sense of drowning brought on by that greeting. Fixing a tight smile on her face, she desperately hoped she'd managed to hide the shock blowing through her at the close-up sight of him. Jack had always been a handsome dude, but three years on and wow. Her fingers tingled. Her stomach crunched. Lust, pure and simple, hot and complex, bubbled through her. Oh, boy, this reunion wasn't supposed to be filled with desire and temptation. Mates, remember? 'To think you're going to be working on the helicopters.'

'Why wouldn't I?' His grin faded. 'I was blown away when I saw *your* name on the staff list. I didn't know you were back in the country, let alone Wellington.' His eyes narrowed as he looked her over with a familiar slow slide down her body that made her blood race and lifted goose-bumps on her skin. Made her want him. Badly.

The whole thing about having to work with Jack had just got monumentally harder. She fought the flare of annoyance that he could make her feel like this so easily after such a long time. 'I know what you mean. To think you'd even consider leaving the emergency department came as a bombshell.' That was the truth.

'I'm full of surprises.' Was that a hint of sarcasm in his tone?

'Maybe I've got a few of my own,' she retorted. Like the house she'd bought and the renovations she was doing to it, like her cute little friend sharing the place with her. If those things didn't astonish Jack then he must have turned to stone over the years she'd been away.

Then a memory swamped her, flattening her with shame.

Three years ago Jack's face had registered shock and disbelief over her biggest surprise ever. 'You're really going? Leaving Wellington? Leaving me?'

'I have to. I'm never going to find my father by staying here, and since I've learned he's American it makes sense to go over to the States. Come on, Jack, try to understand. For the first time ever I've got a starting point. How could I not go?' Her hands had trembled so much she'd dropped her dinner plate and splattered her meal all over the floor. 'You could come with me,' she'd whispered in desperation.

'Sure, Red, just drop everything and leave. Like it's that easy. I've got nearly a year to go before I qualify as an emergency specialist. Stopping in midstream just isn't possible.' He'd taken her cold hands in his. 'You could wait for me.'

She'd shaken her head, beating down the urge to fling herself in his arms and hold on for ever. 'I can't. I've waited all my life to meet my dad and this is the closest I've ever got to finding him. This is so important to me. I have to go.' Jack had been just as important, maybe more, but she'd foolishly believed finding her parent had been paramount.

Jack's face had been bleak, his eyes dark with sadness. 'Until you do this you're never going to be completely happy, are you? Not even with me?'

She hadn't been able to answer him for the lump in her throat.

That was when the arguments had begun, almost as a defence mechanism to protect their shattering hearts. They'd agreed they had to make a clean break but the days before she'd flown out had been intense as they'd crammed as much loving as possible into the little time left.

Now Jack lifted a hand in a stop sign, worry darkening his all-seeing eyes. 'Hey, let's leave the past alone. After all, it isn't called the past for nothing.'

Ouch. 'True. This is a different job; we're probably different people now.' She certainly was. Forcing a smile, she asked, 'So how's life been treating you? You're looking pretty good for an old guy.'

His smoky grey eyes lightened, twinkled, the crinkles at their corners bunching up. That heart-stopping smile lifted his mouth. And cramped her stomach. 'Can't complain. And less of the "old guy" stuff. Turning thirty was an event, not a disaster.'

So why the sudden doubt reflecting back at her? Jack had always been confident, in control. Doubt hadn't even been in his vocabulary. These days she wasn't in a position to ask anything personal. Not that he'd tell her anyway. Talking about the things that bothered him wasn't in his make-up. He took everything life tossed at him and moved on with a nonchalance that hid his true feelings. He was a rock. The person every-one could, and did, rely on in all situations. He didn't ever ask anyone to prop him up.

So she knocked on her head in fun. 'Of course, you've had one of those big birthdays.' She did a quick tap dance on the spot, checked him out. 'I hope that means everything's okay with you, no bits rotting and dropping off your wrinkled old frame.'

'Heck, Red, I've missed your cheek. No one else is ever so damned rude to me.' Suddenly Ruby's feet were off the ground as Jack swung her up against his hard-muscled frame and engulfed her in a bear hug.

'So who's been keeping you in line, then?' she gasped against his chest. His heart pounded under her ear. Strong and steady, like Jack. His arms were muscular and warm around her back. Just like old times. As her bones liquefied with longing, she wriggled to be set free in case she did something dumb like press in against him and hold on for ever.

Jack tightened his grip, but he didn't answer her question. 'You're looking good, girl. Even with that weird spiky hair and the glaring scarlet colour you've dunked it in,' he murmured against her ear, sending thrilling shivers down her spine. 'What happened to that beautiful, sherry-coloured mane?'

It had reminded her of Jack too much. Every time she'd looked in a mirror after they'd broken up her heart had snapped in half all over again. 'It was a nuisance whenever I put my headpiece on in the 'copter.'

'Fair enough.' His disappointed sigh blew against her cheek. His arms tightened further. 'Pity, though.'

She murmured against his jacket, 'You would say that. You didn't have to look after the darned stuff.' But he had spent hours brushing the waist-length hair that had been her one vanity. She quickly added, in case he thought she was stirring up trouble, 'It was a full-time job.'

When his fingers pressed a little harder into her waist Ruby felt a pull of the love they'd once shared. A steady love emanating from Jack's goodness, strength and caring. Added to by her quirky sense of humour and the wonder she'd felt at someone so smart wanting *her*. Not even her beloved mother had made her feel as good, as safe, as Jack had. And just as she'd done with her mother's love, she'd fought that feeling, turned it against herself, shunned Jack's love for her own needs, thereby ruining something very special and worth holding on to at all costs. Hindsight sucked. Big time.

Would she get a second chance?

Ruby breathed Jack in. The scent of pine needles teased her and brought back recollections of long, frenetic afternoons spent making love. So he still wore the same aftershave. What else did he do the same? Was he even the same person? Not if that doubt in his eyes was an indicator.

Then, as suddenly as he'd lifted her into his arms, he plonked her back on the ground. She stumbled as she struggled to maintain her balance. A firm grip on her elbow helped, until a zing of heat spiralled up the inside of her arm, warming the sensitive skin.

'Careful.' His tone was suddenly abrupt.

'Thanks.' Tugging her arm free, she rubbed hard to dissipate the heat he'd so easily generated. Looking up, she found Jack studying her with the same disconcerting expression in those eyes that had haunted her from the moment she'd walked away from him at the airport. The expression that said you didn't know what you had until you lost it. How true that had turned out to be.

Jack jerked his head up, looking beyond them, as though suddenly remembering where he was, who he was talking to. He would soon be in charge of the Wellington Helicopter Rescue base and she was a crew member. 'So you're now a paramedic on the rescue helicopters. That's quite a sideways step from the emergency nurse you desperately wanted to be.'

'Close enough to the same thing. Emergency department, ambulance crew.' Her spread hand flipped left and right. 'No different from what you're doing by taking up this position, I'd have thought.' She strove to avoid what he was really saying: that she never finished anything she started. How could she? She'd always been too busy moving on to stay anywhere long enough to see any project through.

But for the first time in her life she had completed something, something very important to her. A genuine certificate hung on her bedroom wall. Signed by the Chief of Ambulance Services, San Francisco.

Ruby Smith, Advanced Paramedic. Honours. Right alongside the citation for bravery during duty. And on the other side hung the nursing certificate she'd finally obtained in the States.

If only her mother could see those certificates. She'd have been pleased with her daughter for once. The only other person she'd wanted to share her success with at the time now stood in front of her and it was too late. He might know she'd finally qualified at something but he hadn't been there to share in the sheer wonder of achievement. Because of all her stupid mistakes she'd been alone.

From the day she decided to head back here she'd known she'd eventually catch up with Jack. This was the first city she'd ever returned to. She'd come back for Jack, because of Jack. Wellington was Jack. And yet she'd been dragging her heels about calling him. Afraid to find out he'd moved on and barely remembered her.

Ruby closed her eyes briefly. This was way too hard. *Be strong, be tough.* She repeated the mantra that had got her through the last few years, and then diverted the conversation to safe ground. Again.

'I didn't think you were starting with us until next week.' Ruby huffed out a breath and tipped her head back to stare up at him. 'Did I read the wrong memo?'

He grinned that grin, though his eyes were a little slow in keeping up. 'I've been at the aero club for a couple of hours. Since the club's almost next door I figured I'd cruise over here and meet whoever was on duty.'

'Aero club? Your brother still flying those little things?' She glanced across the tarmac at the tiny planes pegged down outside the clubrooms.

'No, Steve's on jumbos these days. It's me who's flying those Tomahawks you're staring at.' A deep chuckle rumbled through him. Another familiar, heart-warming thing she'd missed, desperately at times when she'd been terribly lonely.

'No way.' She grinned as she swivelled back to gape at him. Jack had never had time for play. 'Really? You're learning to fly?'

'And loving every minute I get in the air.' Another chuckle. But it sounded brittle. Something was wrong with this picture. Was happy Jack not really so happy?

'Can you take me up one day?' Bad question. Mouth on the run.

Taking a backward step, Jack told her firmly, 'Sorry, no passengers allowed until I've got my licence.'

He needn't look so relieved. 'How many hours have you flown?'

'Twenty-seven and I need at least fifty before my flight test.' He looked towards the helicopter. 'Want to introduce me?'

Yikes. She'd totally forgotten Dave waiting for her to help tidy up the aircraft's interior. She spun back to the 'copter looming above her, talking to Jack over her shoulder, trying not to stare at his beloved face. 'I thought you two would've met already since it's his job you're taking over.'

'When I came out here with the director, Dave was away on a job.'

'Then you'll both have lots to discuss.' She called up, 'Dave, come out here for a moment. Please.'

Dave poked his head out. 'So how come you didn't kill this guy for calling you Red?'

Because Jack had always called her that. She hated anyone else using the nickname because it tainted her sweet memories of him, and played havoc with the sexy ones as well. 'He's going to be my boss.'

'Didn't stop you reading the Riot Act when I dared to call you Red.' Dave looked across at Jack, then back at her, a hint of worry in his eyes. 'So you two already know each other.' Was he wondering if this would affect the job situation? If it did then Jack could swap crews.

'We worked together once.' In another, totally

different life. Ruby gritted her teeth. 'I was a trainee nurse, Jack was a bossy intern.'

Jack grunted. 'Me? Bossy? I'd have given you that hat, Red.'

'Medicine's a small world.' The older man smiled down at Jack. 'Well, hi, there, anyway, welcome aboard. You're in for some adventures for sure.'

'There'll definitely be some interesting days,' Ruby seconded her partner. Like when the weather was atrocious and any flying became scary. She never admitted to those fears, just tightened her harness and pretended nothing was wrong. Now she officially introduced the two men. 'Dave, this is Jack Forbes.' She watched them size each other up in a man kind of way as they reached to shake hands.

They must've decided the other was okay because within moments Dave handed down the packs to Ruby and invited Jack on board for a cursory rundown on how things worked.

'I'll leave you two to it,' Ruby said as she slung one pack over her shoulders. 'When I've topped these up, I'll put a brew on.' And finally get to eat that pie. It'd be cold and congealed but right now it made her mouth water and her stomach expand with hope.

Jack reached for the second heavy bag. 'I'll take this one in for you.'

Ruby grabbed it out of his hand. The bags were heavy but she never, ever let the men carry them for her, even on the days her damaged knee played up. Hauling them was part of her job. 'I'm fine with it. Dave's got lots to show you.'

'I'm not a greenhorn, Red. I've done the training, know where everything is kept, how to activate the winch, how to use the radio.' Exasperation tinged his voice.

'Still, each 'copter has a slightly different configuration. You might as well take a look with Dave while it's quiet.'

Jack shook his head. 'And I thought I was in charge.'

'Not until tomorrow.' Ruby winked at him. 'And only once you've been out for three retrievals.'

Not entirely true but the crews checked out a newbie on the first few trips before accepting him or her completely. Being an A and E specialist with loads of experience wouldn't save his backside. Working with the limited resources they carried in the helicopter was very different from being in a fully equipped emergency department, not to mention the situations they often found themselves in.

Ruby saw a frown developing on Jack's forehead. He'd hate her telling him to take a back seat, but he'd better get used to it. The other crew members would be tougher.

His eyes narrowed. 'Three? First I've heard of it.'

'Don't tell me that you didn't keep an eye on any new staff in the emergency department?'

'Of course I did. It goes with the territory,' he snapped.

Where had that come from? 'Relax, we're a friendly lot. You'll be a perfect fit in our team.'

Jack blinked, flexed and shook his hands, loosened his shoulders, then pushed a cautious smile across his mouth. 'You're presuming I haven't taken up any edgy hobbies lately.'

'You betcha.' One thing she could be sure of, he didn't do edgy. Except he was now learning to fly. For Jack, that really was putting himself out there, a bit like hanging off a cliff on a dodgy rope. Who was this Jack? She didn't entirely recognise him and yet he looked the same. More mature, more handsome, sexier than ever but still the same. Yet something was different. That flicker of doubt in his eyes, that sudden annoyance with her, for starters.

Maybe she was looking too hard. More likely he was reacting to seeing her again. Not easy for either of them.

Ruby headed for the hangar before she got tangled up in trying to solve the puzzle. The next four months would give her plenty of time to sort Jack out. Not to mention her own mixed-up feelings towards him.

Jack's hands gripped his hips as he watched Red lug those bags across the tarmac. She displayed all the nonchalance of a weightlifter. Her slight, short frame was taut, her boots heavy as they trod the concrete. She'd already got to him. Anger flared quickly, fizzed along his veins. This was supposed to be the start of a whole new life for him, not a revisiting of the old one. He'd broken his heart over her once. That had been bad luck. To let it happen again would be plain careless.

If he had known she was back in town, would he have quit his Head of Department position? Damn right he would have. Ruby had long given up the right to alter his life decisions. And this job was the result of those decisions.

He tossed caution aside, and called, 'Hey, Red, I'm going to give you a hand.'

She turned slowly, balancing carefully, smiling widely, fixedly. 'Got two perfectly good ones of my own, thanks.'

A familiar 'don't fool with me' look had snapped into her big green eyes. Was it because he dared to question her capabilities? Was she more confident these days? Or better at hiding her insecurities?

Jack tried to grin back. He didn't do so well. 'That was my last offer.'

'No worries.'

Was she favouring her left leg? 'Did you jar your leg when you jumped down? You look like you're limping.'

Her smile tightened further, warning lights switched on in those piercing eyes. 'I'm perfectly fit, thank you.'

'I don't doubt you are but I'm allowed to show

an interest in my colleagues.' With a fierce flick of his shoulders he filed her limp in the dossier in his mind. For now. Remain aloof with her. Do not get involved. Was there a textbook on how to behave around ex-girlfriends?

'She's a tough one,' Dave said behind him. 'Doesn't like any of the men singling her out to give her a break with some of the heavy stuff.'

Huh? Since when? 'Ruby wasn't always like that.' Jack clambered inside the gleaming red helicopter. 'Guess I don't know her as well as I used to,' he added as he looked around the compact interior. At last the excitement he was supposed to feel for this job began leaking into him.

'People change,' Dave muttered.

Jack winced. Yeah, that was exactly why he was here instead of running the emergency department. 'I'm sure we'll get along just fine.'

Dave said, 'Funny thing but Ruby's tough-girl attitude actually makes all of us try to do more for her than you'd normally expect. On and off base. All the crews are close, and we spend a lot of time together, but with Ruby we seem to go those extra miles, if you know what I mean?'

'I'll keep that in mind.' And keep my distance.

Going the extra mile might take him a lot closer to Red than was healthy for his future plans. Or for his body if his overheated reaction when he'd held her minutes ago was anything to go by. How would he put distance between them when they were stuffed inside this cramped area?

'Good.' Dave turned back to the stretcher he was cleaning.

Jack studied the man he'd be relieving. 'You worried I'll have scared her off by the time you come back?' Ruby would go, but not because of him. Moving on was her modus operandi. Ironic that soon he would be heading away too.

'We've got an excellent group of very professional people working here now and I'd hate to see the status quo change. If my wife hadn't gone and bought our tickets and booked our tours, I probably wouldn't be going to Europe this year.' Dave's brow creased. 'Which is why Gail did it, of course. Women are very crafty, aren't they?'

'They can be.' But not Red. She was more like a moth continuously flying at the light, getting nowhere. Always a tight coil of tense muscles with a sharp tongue to match. Jack used to wind her up just so they could kiss and make up later.

He'd be wise to remember that in the weeks to come and ignore any outbursts. There'd be no making up now. Forget those heady kisses, the hottest sex he'd ever experienced and a lot of plain old fun and laughter. Forget how she could melt into absolute sweetness at the most unexpected moments.

Start with remembering her name was Ruby. Not Red. And that she wasn't his type of woman. He took another glance outside, his eyes tracking the one woman he'd ever cared about. His gut twisted. Red's sassy butt still swayed saucily. Sex in boots. Hot sex in a jumpsuit. 'It's been a while.'

Since he'd seen her. Since he'd held her in his arms and kissed her senseless. Since— Stop. Tormenting himself would only lead to trouble. But she'd felt wonderful when he'd lifted her up against his chest minutes ago. Warm, lithe, exciting.

'Odd that she didn't mention knowing you.' Dave's words crashed into his brain, slamming him back to reality.

Words that stung. Hard and deep. He shouldn't be surprised. When he and Red agreed to split they'd both made it perfectly clear there'd be no going back on their decision. But surely that hadn't meant they couldn't acknowledge one another. 'It was a few years ago. How long has she been working with you?'

'Two months. Came straight from San Francisco.'

'Two months?' Jack all but shouted. If Ruby had kicked him in the guts it couldn't have hurt any worse. Two months and not a word. Talk about putting him in his place. Sensing Dave's eagle eye on him, he bit down on the oath hovering on the tip of his tongue and tried for casually unconcerned. 'I've got a lot of catching up to do with her.' But not on this shift.

'She certainly has great work experience. Her credentials are superb.'

'It's the first time Ruby's actually stuck at anything long enough to qualify.' Amazing. And as far as he knew it was also the first time she'd returned anywhere. Had she finally tracked down her father and dealt with the past? That was the only explanation for her spending long enough in one place to put in the required hours to become a paramedic. Did that mean her angst had disappeared? Did a dog suddenly grow wool on its back?

Jack asked, 'Is Ruby still taking on everyone head first? Like she has to knock them down before they get to her?' He shouldn't be asking Dave, but he was speaking boss to boss here, needing to know about a member of his crew.

Believe that and he'd believe anything.

Dave studied him thoughtfully. Was he having doubts about leaving his job in Jack's hands? 'Can't say as I've noticed. And working in stressful situations on a daily basis I think I would've. Is that the Ruby you used to know?'

Already regretting his question, Jack nodded. He'd hate for Dave to think differently of Ruby because of him. 'She used to have a few issues that distressed her big time but from what you're saying maybe she's sorted them out.'

'Some relationships don't stand the test of time, do they?' Dave was studying him with a glint in his eye suggesting he'd somehow be watching out for Ruby even from afar, making sure his replacement didn't upset her. Nice to know she had such a good friend. The man hadn't finished. 'But others can.'

Shaking his head, Jack muttered, 'Not this one.'

Dave shrugged. 'That's a shame. I get the feeling Ruby's ready to settle down.'

'Then you really don't know her.' Ruby didn't do settling down. Ever. Not like him. He'd been happy to stay in this place where he'd lived all his life. Until recently. Now he was so restless he itched. He was on the move, done with being the man everyone relied on to be a permanent fixture for them, of always being around when others found their lives going pear-shaped. It was time for his own adventures, and no one, not even a certain scarlet-haired woman, was going to upset this. *Look out, world, Jack Forbes is coming. Yeah, right.*

Jack forced a smile as he continued to watch her disappearing inside. She was as sexy as ever. His body had recognised her instantly. That slow burn starting in the pit of his belly when he'd seen her in the helicopter. And now it had spread out, down and up, engulfing every cell of his body. He wanted her. As strongly as he always had. *Great to see ya, ruby-red girl.*

Enough. Just seeing Red made him reel. Why he'd lifted her into that hug was beyond him, but nothing could've stopped him when she'd dropped to the ground right in front of him. To feel her body along the length of his, to touch that spiky hair with his chin, had brought longing charging through him. He flicked his finger against his thumb. *Dumb ass.*

So much for keeping everything on a boss to crew member basis. Should he hug every member? For a brief moment with Ruby in his arms he'd felt as though they'd never been apart. As if all that pain hadn't happened, hadn't torn him into shreds.

Jack turned and deliberately began studying the interior of the aircraft that would become a big part of his life for the next few months. 'It's a bit of a squeeze.'

Dave grinned. 'Takes some getting used to.'

'And I'm always at the front,' a man drawled from the other side of the bulkhead. 'Along with Slats. He's ducked into the hangar for a minute.'

Dave grinned. 'Chris, get through here and meet Jack.' To Jack he said, 'This guy is one hell of a pilot. You want him with you when the sky's full of bumps.'

Jack shook hands with the man who didn't look old enough to have left school let alone know how to fly one of these massive helicopters. 'Good to meet you. How many hours have you done on this bird?'

Chris laughed. 'More than you'd ever believe. For the record, I stopped drinking milk thirty years ago.'

The man had to be pulling his leg. The same age as him? Nah, couldn't be. But Chris looked like he meant it. 'Bet you have to produce your ID every time you buy a beer.'

'Damned pain at times,' Dave muttered. 'But that innocent face pulls the girls, make no mistake.'

Jack could believe it. What about Ruby? Was she a fan of the pilot? As in had she been out with him, been to bed with him? A cold knot formed in Jack's belly. There had to be a man in her life. A very attractive, sexy woman always had a man, and Red was both. But it wasn't his place to comment, despite the chill creeping over his skin. Red was a free agent. Like him. The fact that they were going to work together again didn't give him any rights over who she went out with. *So behave, Jacko.*

Jack dragged his hand down his cheek. As her

boss, he had to learn about her situation, as he did for all the staff. If anyone's private life was out of sync over anything at all he'd want to know about it. Happy staff meant a happy work environment, which in turn meant everyone pulled together to give an exceptionally good service to the public.

Just remember her name was Ruby, not Red, and he should be able to keep everything in perspective. Haa!

CHAPTER TWO

JULIE, the part-time office lady, stood in the middle of the hangar, staring over at the helicopter. 'So who's the hottie?'

Ruby grinned at her. 'Jack Forbes.'

'As in Dave's replacement? No way. He's got a body to die for. And that face, that grin…' Julie spluttered to a halt, her eyes enormous.

Ruby shook her head. 'Too hot to handle?'

Flapping her hands at her cheeks, Julie replied, 'Remind me to bring my oven mitts to work tomorrow.'

'Got two pairs?' There was no point denying Jack's good looks. That would only make people question her ability to see.

'Guess you'll need them more than me, since you'll be working alongside him. Wonder what he's like behind those looks?'

'Imperturbable,' she muttered. Gorgeous, funny, trustworthy, lovable Jack.

'You already know him?' Julie's perfectly styled eyebrows rose as she continued to stare in the direction of the helicopter.

'From the days when I was training to be a nurse.' She'd spent seven months in Wellington, on her way from Nelson to somewhere else, which, on the death of her mother, had turned out to be Seattle. Her training had spread over four cities, and had to be the most erratic on record.

'You weren't an item? You know, had a doctors-and-nurses thing going on?'

They'd certainly had something going on, something very hot. Don't forget the love. There'd been plenty of that too. But not enough to keep them together. What if she was incapable of loving someone enough to get through all the things that got tossed up along the way?

She shuddered, shoved that idea out of the way and said to Julie, 'If I didn't know how happily married you were, I'd be arranging a date for you with Jack.' If he wasn't already in a relationship with the stunning, lithe blonde Ruby had seen him with in a café four weeks ago. Blondie had been as close to Jack as sticking plaster, and he hadn't been objecting. Ruby tripped on an uneven piece of concrete. Her knee jagged. She sucked air through her teeth and swore to be more careful.

Julie chuckled. 'Looking's fine. It's the touching that gets people into trouble.'

Ruby winced. Didn't she know it? Touching Jack had always led to a lot of up-close involvement, a conflagration, so there'd be absolutely no touching this time round. Huge problems lurked there that she wasn't ready to face. Jack was her past, no matter how much she suddenly wished otherwise. She'd hurt him once, she wouldn't do that to him again. Or to herself. She headed the subject to safer ground. 'How come you're here on a Sunday?'

Julie told her, 'I'm taking tomorrow morning off so I can go on a school trip with my girls. There's a pile of reports that need filing with the health department before Wednesday so here I am.'

'I'd better get these bags sorted.' Ruby reached the storeroom, exhaling the breath she'd been holding while studying Jack. The sight of him made her giddy, while being near him, being held in that embrace, had made her feel somehow complete. As only Jack had ever made her feel. Damn him. If she'd stayed in Wellington way back then she'd have saved herself a lot of anguish with her father. *And* she'd still be in a relationship with Jack.

Or would she? They'd both had a lot of personal issues to sort out that might've strained their relationship to the point it couldn't survive. Could be they'd both needed to grow up. Ruby blinked. Definitely true of her. Not so sure about Jack. Did he still resent his father for leaning too hard on him for support? How strange that set-up had been. Parents were supposed to look out for their kids, not the other way round. But of course Jack had never gone into any detail about his family so she only had half the story.

Grabbing at airway tubes, she quickly topped up the bags, while musing on the past. Staying put in one place had been an alien concept for her. That she'd even considered stopping here three years ago spoke volumes about her feelings for Jack. But in the end the forces that had driven her relentlessly onward all her life had won out. Not even for the love of her life, Jack, could she have given up something that had eaten at her as far back as she could recall.

Julie stood in the doorway. 'You planning on smashing those vials or what?'

Ruby looked at the replacement drugs she'd just rammed into their slots. 'Guess not.'

'Mr Gorgeous has got to you already, hasn't he?'

Unfortunately, yes. 'I'll get over it. You wanted me for something?'

'Can you translate Jason's writing for me?' Julie held a report form out to her. 'Sometimes I wonder if medical staff do a 101 course in Scribble.'

'Doctors say it's because they're always frantically busy.' At least that was what Jack used to tell her.

Jack. Jack. Jack. Suddenly everything came back to him. Already there was no avoiding him. It was so unfair. She'd come here first, this was her job, her sanctuary. There were plenty of places out there for an emergency specialist to work. *Why pick this one, Jack?* Despair crunched inside her. It was hard enough getting her life on track and keeping it there, without the added difficulty of having to spend twelve hours a day with a man who knew the old Ruby. And who was going to struggle to believe the new version she'd made herself into—if he'd even take the time to get to know her again. And suddenly she really, really wanted him to.

Julie laughed. 'That's a cop-out. But, then, most people blame texting for their appalling spelling too. Lazy, I reckon.' She turned for her office. 'I've put the kettle on.'

'Ta. I'll tell the guys.' Ruby cringed. A cop-out. Her father had come up with a million reasons for never coming to New Zealand to meet her, all of them cop-outs. If only she'd believed her mother, whom she'd badgered incessantly all her life for more information about the airman she'd imagined to be a hero. But her mother had only ever said Ruby was better off not knowing him.

As a child Ruby had waited for him to turn up bearing gifts and hugs. He would tell her he was home for good and that they'd have a happy life doing all the things her mother couldn't afford to do. Not until she'd packed up her mother's home after her death did Ruby learn her dad was American and had been in the US Air Force. Her parents had met when her father's plane had stopped in Christchurch for a few days on the way to Antarctica.

Finally it hadn't been too difficult to finally track down the man who'd spawned her. Reality had been harsh. The hero of her childhood had turned out to be a total nightmare. Her humiliation at her father's lifestyle equalled her embarrassment at how badly she'd treated her mother over the years. Then had come the acute disappointment at the realisation she'd given up Jack for that man.

The Greaser—she no longer called him her father—was a good-looking man who'd used his abundant charm to marry into a fortune and produce offspring to keep everyone onside, especially his wealthy father-in-law, while he philandered his way through half his town's women.

Outside, Ruby heaved one of the replenished packs up into the helicopter. 'Kettle's boiled.' At last she'd get to eat that sorry-looking pie. Her stomach rolled over in happy anticipation.

Jack took the pack and strapped it into place. 'We're about done in here.'

She bent down for the other bag, grimacing as she lifted the heavy weight up.

'Here, give me that.' Jack reached down and took the load from her, his fingers brushing hers.

Instant heat sizzled up her arms. Clenching her hands at her sides, she spoke too loudly. 'Thanks. It goes—'

'Over there by the stretcher,' Jack finished with a growl, his eyebrows nearly meeting in the middle of his forehead. His gaze appeared stuck on a spot behind her head while shock flicked through his eyes. So he'd felt the same sparks too. The sparks that made everything so much more difficult.

'Glad you've got it sussed.' It was important. If any equipment got put away in the wrong place, it could delay things in an emergency.

'It's not rocket science.' A glint in his eye warned her he wasn't happy with her telling him anything about the helicopter.

'You didn't used to be so touchy.' But he had touched her often.

Jack dropped down beside her, and unsure of him, she tensed, waiting for him to bawl her out, ready to meet him head on. Instead he stole the breath from her by saying, 'So, a paramedic, eh? Did you ever finish your nursing certificate?'

'Advanced paramedic, actually.'

'Sorry, advanced paramedic.' His eyebrows rose. 'That's fantastic. I'm glad you qualified. You certainly have the smarts.'

She straightened a little at his compliment. 'Yes, I did finish the year on the wards required to finalise my nurse's practising certificate.' She'd worked extremely hard to get all her qualifications. Not being satisfied with a pass, she'd aimed for the highest grades possible. That had been the first good turning point in her life. Jack could raise his eyebrows all he liked but he wouldn't dent her pride in her accomplishments. 'I trained on the ambulances in San Francisco. Then during the last four months there I took a rotation on the rescue helicopters, which stood me in good stead for this job.' She'd found her niche. Nothing, nobody would make her give it up. Not a bung knee. Definitely not Jack.

'San Francisco, eh?' His tone was acid and he stared straight ahead as they walked towards the hangar and the staffrooms.

Beside him she grinned, refusing to be intimidated by his attitude. He might think he still knew her but, boy, oh, boy, he didn't have a clue.

She'd returned to Wellington, this time permanently. This was the first city in a long line of cities that she'd come back to. Might as well get some of the details out of the way, let him have his 'I told you so' moment. 'I started in Seattle, then went to Vancouver. I really loved Canada but couldn't get a job without a work permit. Back in the States I headed down to Kansas, LA, San Diego and finally San Francisco.' She wasn't going to enlighten him about her reasons for all that tripping around. Not yet anyway. Not unless they got past being mates. Which, right now, looked doubtful. *Unfortunately.*

'When did you find time to fit in your training?' Strong acid.

'I lived in San Fran for two years, ample time to qualify. My nursing training put me ahead on the course when I started on the ambulance.' And she'd focused entirely on her job, no sexy distractions anywhere in sight.

'Two years in one spot?' The acid sweetened up a little. 'Did you ever come back here for a visit?'

'No. Too busy.' And, because they'd agreed their break-up was final, there'd been nothing, no one, to come back for.

'Where are you living now?'

'I bought a villa on Mount Victoria.' Glancing sideways, she saw his eyebrows lift, his lips tighten, and she braced herself.

His words dripped sarcasm. 'Don't tell me you're settling down? Not you. Come on, I bet you've still got that backpack in the corner of your wardrobe, waiting for the day you've had enough of Wellington.'

'Long gone, fallen apart from overuse.' Not a great testament to her reliability. But, 'I'm renovating the house. It's so out of date and colder than an iceberg now that winter's here. The electricity and plumbing need completely redoing, not to mention the antiquated kitchen and a bathroom requiring a total refit.' All of which were already guzzling up cash like a thirsty dog.

'You haven't exactly answered my question. How long do you think you'll be around this time?' His mouth was still tight, but his eyebrows were back in place. 'You never showed any interest in owning a house. Too much of a tie, you reckoned, if I recall correctly.'

Which, of course, he did. But that had been aeons ago. And deep down she had wanted a home but fear of not being able to make a success of it had driven her to deny the need. What had she ever known about setting up a permanent home? Continuing to ignore his underlying disbelief, she said, 'The villa's eighty-nine years old, and showing its age. But I love it. There's so much potential.'

'Oh, right. You'll be here until you've done the house up. A quick lick of paint? Some new carpet?' He held the door to the staff kitchen open for her. 'Can't quite picture you as a house renovator.'

'Give me a break. I've never had the opportunity before.' And they both knew that had been her fault.

Behind her Dave piped up. 'Ruby's a dab hand at pulling down walls. You should see her swinging a hammer.'

'That's the best bit,' she agreed, grateful for Dave's support.

Jack peered down at her. 'You do know what you're doing, Ruby? Has a builder looked over your plans? Or are you leaping in feet first and knocking out parts of the house any old how?

You could bring the roof down on your head if you take out a load-bearing wall.'

'Tea or coffee?' she asked sweetly, fighting the urge to hit him. Of course she knew what she was doing. 'I have expert help.' Chris had been a builder until he'd decided there had to be more excitement to life and learned to fly helicopters. He'd been more than happy to take a look at the house and tell her what she could and couldn't do to it. He'd also put her in touch with a reliable draughtsman who fully understood her need to keep the house in period while modernising the essentials.

'Coffee, thanks.' Jack dropped onto a chair at the table. Questions still clouded his eyes.

'Dave, Chris?' Outside, the rotors of the second rescue helicopter began slowing down. Ruby got out more mugs for the other crew. 'Where's Slats?'

'Right here.' A short, wiry man sauntered in and handed Dave some paperwork.

Chris sat down and introduced Jack to his offsider before returning to the previous conversation. 'Ruby's got everything under control with the house, Jack. We made sure of that the moment we learned what she was up to. She's one very organised lady. And damned determined when she sets her mind to something.'

'Here you go.' Ruby slid the filled mugs across the table towards the men.

Jack's eyebrows were on the move again. 'Ruby? Organised?' His eyes widened and he turned to her. 'Have you had a total mind make-over since I saw you last?' He certainly didn't have any hang-ups about everyone knowing they used to know each other.

'Sort of.' She shrugged off his criticism. 'I definitely don't rush things like a sprinter out of the starter's block any more.'

Jack told Chris, 'Three years ago, if she'd wanted a wall taken out, she'd have taken it out, regardless of load bearing or any other constraints.'

Chris laughed. 'Sometimes it's hard to slow Ruby down once she gets going with that mallet, but she's very conscious of making the best out of this house. It's going to be well worth all her efforts.'

Jack pressed his lips together. Holding back a retort? Then he headed to the sink, poured the coffee away and began making another one. Without milk.

'Oh, sorry.' She'd made it the way he used to drink it. Silly girl. She should've asked, not presumed, she knew.

'Not a problem.'

Leaning back against the small bench, Ruby folded her arms over her abdomen, holding her mug in one hand. Her pie was heating in the microwave. She put distance between her and Jack, all too aware of the sparks that would fly if they touched. Trying not to watch as he stirred the bottom out of his coffee mug was hard after all those years of wondering about him; yearning for his touch, his kisses, even his understanding. She remembered how those long fingers now holding the teaspoon used to trip lightly over her feverish skin, sensitising her from head to toe.

He glanced over. 'What?'

'Nothing.' Thoughtlessly she laid a hand on his upper arm then snatched it back as his eyebrows rose. Dropping onto a chair, she surreptitiously continued to study him over the rim of her mug. There were a few more crinkles at the corners of his eyes, an occasional grey strand on his head. His tall frame still didn't carry any excess weight, but when he'd held her he'd felt more muscular than before. Had he started working out? In a gym? Not likely. But, then, how was she to know?

On her belt the pager squawked out a message, as it did on Dave's. He said, 'I'll get the details.'

'Damn it, when do I get to eat?' She spun around to empty her coffee into the sink and bumped into Jack. As she snatched the microwave open, she clamped down on the sweet shivers dancing over her skin. 'Lukewarm's better than no pie at all,' she muttered, before sinking her teeth into the gluggy pastry and racing for the helicopter behind Chris and Slats. Would lukewarm Jack be better than no Jack at all? At least she was getting away from him, and he'd have gone by the time they got back.

As Ruby clambered up into the 'copter Dave called out, 'You're picking up a cardiac arrest patient from the inter-island ferry.' He came closer, Jack on his heels. 'Ruby, I'm sending Jack in my place. Show him the ropes, will you?'

'Sure,' she spluttered. Didn't anyone around here listen to her? Couldn't they hear her silent pleas? She did not want to be confined inside the 'copter with Jack until she'd had a few days to get her mixed-up emotions under control. Her heart thudded against her ribs. Would that even be possible?

Toughen up and deal with it. Deal with Jack. He was here. That was all there was to it. Her chin jutted out and her spine clicked as she straightened unnaturally tight and upright. She'd do the job, show him the ropes, and then she was due two days' leave.

Out over Cook Strait, Chris hovered the helicopter above the rolling deck of the inter-islander. The sky was clear and cold, the sea running fast with a big swell. Not ideal but it could've been a whole lot worse.

'Send the stretcher after me,' Ruby instructed Jack as she prepared to be lowered to the deck with a pack and the oxygen bottle on her back.

'Right,' Jack snapped.

So he thought he should go first. Tough. It was her job today. At least he hadn't argued and wasted valuable time. That was the Jack she remembered.

The ship lurched upwards as her feet reached for the deck, jarring her whole body and giving her knee some grief. Mindful of the ship's crew, she swore silently and tried hard not to limp as she crossed to her patient, checking the area for any obstacles that might get in the way of the stretcher being lowered. She waved the crowd of onlookers further back.

A woman looked up as Ruby crouched uncomfortably beside her. 'I'm a GP. This is Ron Jefferies, fifty years old. Lucky for him I was close by when he fell. I started CPR within sixty seconds. The ferry crew supplied a defibrillator, which I used at maximum joules. We now have a thready heart rhythm.'

Ruby introduced herself as she unzipped the pack and removed an LMA kit. 'Ron, I'm going to insert a tube in your throat and place a mask over your face to give you oxygen.'

'I'll put an IV in.' Jack was down already and knelt opposite.

'Please.' Ruby was already pushing up Ron's sleeve and passing the bag of saline to the GP now standing behind her. Holding the bag aloft helped the fluid flow more easily until they were ready to winch their patient on board the helicopter. She and Jack worked quickly and efficiently together, unfolding the stretcher and snapping the locks into place at the hinges.

She directed Jack and the GP to grip Ron's legs and upper arm, while opposite them she clutched handfuls of his trousers and shirt, ready to pull. 'On the count of three. One. Two. Three.' And their patient was on the stretcher, being belted securely.

'We're ready to transfer.' Ruby spoke to Slats through her mouthpiece as she checked Jack had attached the winch to the stretcher. Within minutes they were all aboard and Chris had headed the machine for Wellington and the hospital.

Jack checked their patient's vitals while Ruby wrote up the patient report form.

'He's one lucky man,' she murmured. 'How often does a GP witness an arrest? Getting the compressions that quickly definitely saved him.'

'He owes her his life for sure.' Jack glanced up at her. 'Did you get her name?'

'No time for that.'

'We didn't learn anything about our man here

either, apart from who he is. I wonder if he was travelling with family? Friends?'

She shook her head. 'According to the steward I spoke to while you were being winched up, he'd put it over the loudspeaker for anyone travelling with Ron Jefferies to come forward, but no one appeared. It will be up to the hospital to track down relatives.'

'They'll be able to talk to him when they remove the LMA.'

'Maybe.' The man didn't look very alert. Ruby watched as Jack rechecked all his vitals.

In her headphone Slats said, 'We're here, folks. The team's waiting for your patient.'

Jack glanced up. 'Thank goodness. Ron needs a cardiologist urgently.'

It didn't take long to hand Ron over to the hospital emergency staff, and then the pilots were skimming across the harbour to the airport and back to base.

Usually Ruby would gaze out the window during this short flight, looking at all the city landmarks, enjoying the moods of the harbour, unwinding after an operation. But now her eyes were drawn to Jack as he sat, hunched in the bucket seat, reading the clinical-procedures note-book they all carried.

Had he missed her as much as she had him?

Jack glanced across to her, a wry expression in those eyes. 'Did I pass my first test?'

She held her hand out flat and wiggled it side to side. 'Maybe.'

Annoyance flickered across his face. 'I'm being serious, Ruby. You made it abundantly clear you'd be checking me out, so I've the right to know what you're going to tell Dave when we're back on the ground.'

Whoa. Who was this angry guy? No one she knew. For someone who wanted to be mates he didn't seem to understand when she was teasing him. 'I couldn't fault you. Okay?' It had been a straightforward job but she refrained from point-ing that out.

'Thank you.' He studied her for a long moment before returning to reading the notebook in his hand.

Prickly so-and-so. Jack would have to learn ev-eryone on the base teased each other every op-portunity they got. It helped ease the stress levels. Pulling the boss card wouldn't keep Jack safe at all, but he could learn that from the others. Right now she wanted out of this confined space so she could breath some Jack-less air, could look in any direction and not have her sight filled with a hunky, mouth-watering vision, could move without fear of bumping into him.

As the helicopter settled gently on the ground and the rotors slowed she stood and ran her hands down her thighs, ready for a quick escape.

'Do we need to take that bag inside to top up or is it all right for me to bring out replacement equipment?' Jack asked.

Peering down at him, Ruby was disconcerted to find him watching her rubbing her thighs. Tucking her hands behind her back, she answered quickly, 'It's fine to bring what's needed out here as long as it's done immediately.' Did he remember smoothing her thighs, running exquisite circles on her skin with his forefinger? Why would he, when she'd only just remembered?

'Then that's what I'll do,' he snapped back. Unlocking the door, he dropped to the ground and strode towards the hangar.

Ruby lowered herself down, mindful of her now throbbing knee. Sucking in her stomach, she concentrated on walking without limping and trying to force Jack out of her mind.

Except he wouldn't go away. She'd angered him again. Since when had he had such a short fuse? He'd been the one to tell jokes and tease people, and had happily accepted the same in return. Had something happened to him during the time she'd been away? Had someone hurt him? Apart from her? Another woman? Ruby stumbled. He could be married by now—to Blondie. No wedding ring meant nothing. Not all men wore them. He was very desirable and she hadn't been the only nurse to set her sights on him in the A and E department. A smug smile tugged at her mouth. She'd been the one to win him, though. Her smile flicked off. That was then. Now was different. He wouldn't let her close a second time.

The sound of her pager snapped through her thoughts. 'Here we go again.' Reading the details coming through, she turned back to the helicopter and clambered inside.

Jack was right behind her, breathing heavily. He slammed the door shut and dropped onto the seat he'd only moments before vacated. 'What have we got?'

Ruby pushed to the front and read back the details coming through on the electronic screen. "'MTV on the Rumataka Road. Female, thirty years, minor injuries but trapped. Stat two. Female, six years, serious facial injuries, possible brain injury. Stat four.'"

'Do we pick them both up? Or just the child?' Jack asked.

'Just the child at this stage. Being a status four, we can't afford to wait until the mother is freed. The mother will be transferred to Hutt Hospital by road.'

'Will we take the child to Hutt Hospital or back to Wellington?'

'It's not our call, but most likely Wellington, where they've got an excellent neurological department. It's only a few minutes' extra flying time.'

'Every minute can count.' Jack's eyes darkened. 'More than anything else, that mother's going to want to be with her daughter.' He twisted around to stare out the window, his hands clenching and unclenching on his thighs, his mouth a white line in his pale face.

'Jack?' Ruby leaned closer, put a hand over his.

What was wrong? It couldn't be the flying, he'd been okay on the last trip, and anyway he was training to be a private pilot.

'I'm fine.' He slid his hand out from under hers, and continued staring outside.

If she hadn't been looking so hard she wouldn't have seen the way his bottom lip quivered ever so slightly. 'Sure.' She had no idea how to get him to open up. Once she'd stupidly thought that if Jack had something to say he'd say it, but now she realised he'd never told her anything that involved his feelings.

Minutes ticked by. Then he coughed. 'I always struggle with seeing kids injured.' His fingers flexed, fisted, flexed.

'I think we all do.' Ruby thought back to when she'd worked alongside Jack in A and E. Had they ever worked together with a seriously sick child? Her mind threw up a memory from her first week in A and E with Dr Forbes.

'Ruby, for God's sake, hurry up with that suction. This kid's going to choke to death.' Jack whipped the tube out of her hand. 'Turn it on. Now.' He whisked the end of the hard plastic around the little boy's mouth, gentle but firm,

sucking up the blood and mucus that filled the cavity. 'Damn it, kid, don't you die on me now.'

Nurses worked around them, stemming blood loss from the child's legs and head, cutting away clothes and ordering X-rays. Ruby smarted as she tossed the boy's now useless trousers into the rubbish bin. She'd reacted instantly to Jack's command to suction the boy's mouth. What was his problem? 'I was doing just fine,' she snapped at him. 'I can take over now.'

'Press on that leg wound. It's bleeding again.' Jack continued suctioning, his fingers unsteady and his mouth a white line in his pale face. He issued orders to the senior nurse about getting the oxygen mask ready, ignoring Ruby.

Later that night, when they knocked off work, Jack said, 'You've got to learn not to answer back in those situations. Whatever I say goes. Understand?'

She'd nodded. 'Sure.' But she'd been shocked at the way he'd snatched that tube out of her hand.

'Ruby, we can always discuss a case after-wards.' He turned for the door, spun back. 'You *did well in there. If I seemed a little abrupt I have my reasons.'*

He'd never told her what those reasons were. That had been before they'd got together so she'd put his reticence down to not knowing her very well. Wrong. It was just how he was. Had something dreadful happened to Jack as a trainee? Had he lost a patient in circumstances he blamed himself for?

In her ear Chris's voice was an abrupt interruption. 'ETA one minute. I'll land on the road above the crash site.'

'Right.' Ruby prepared to leave the helicopter the instant it was possible.

As they raced towards the squashed car, their packs banging heavily on their backs, oxygen tank and defib in Jack's hands, Ruby checked him out. She sighed with relief. Whatever had been disturbing him had gone, replaced with a professional, caring expression and the urgent need to help the little girl they were there for.

A policeman lifted the tape protecting the scene from the crowd of onlookers for Ruby and Jack to duck under. 'I think you're wanted at the ambulance.'

Changing direction, they crossed to the paramedics, who were working with a small patient on a stretcher. Ruby's heart ached when she saw the small, blood-soaked child. A quick look at Jack but, apart from a whitening of his face, he was in full control of himself.

They listened carefully to an ambulance officer's report. 'I've given her a second bolus of saline as her BP keeps dropping. GCS is nine. She's got a poor airway and I couldn't intubate.'

A Glasgow coma score of nine. They didn't come worse than that and the patient still be alive.

'Upgrade to stat five.' Jack immediately opened his pack and reached for a small-sized LMA kit. Ruby took the child's head and tipped it back slightly to allow Jack easier access to her throat. Together they quickly had the airway open and oxygen flowing. Jack's expertise was impressive, and Ruby enjoyed working with him. The girl was in excellent hands.

But as Ruby began to relax, the child went into spasms. A seizure was common with her injuries but distressing for everyone observing it. Other than making sure the girl didn't choke, there was nothing Ruby could do but hold the child's bloodied hand in her gloved one until she fell still again.

After a fast but thorough examination they transferred the girl to the helicopter. As Jack began taking her vitals again, she had another seizure. Followed minutes later by another. And another.

'We'll give her a sedative intra-nasally,' he instructed Ruby as the rotors began speeding up.

Ruby held the nasal cannula in place and talked quietly. 'Come on, sweetheart. This will stop those nasty fits.'

'Blood pressure's dropping.' Jack's voice was calm, steady.

'Stay with us, sweetheart.' *Chris, spin those rotors faster, we need a hospital right now.* 'I wonder what your name is. No one back at the accident scene knew. I bet it's something pretty.'

Jack checked the oxygen saturation level, adjusted the flow from the tank. Took blood-pressure readings again, counted the little girl's respiratory rate.

Ruby, uncharacteristically feeling totally helpless, called up Wellington Hospital Emergency Department and gave them the child's medical details and their ETA. They were doing all they could but it was nowhere near enough.

Slats's calm voice sounded in her headset. 'One minute to touchdown.'

A team of paediatric doctors and nurses awaited them, moving towards the helicopter the moment Ruby shoved the door open. The transfer was made with such care that Ruby felt an urge to cry and had to squash it down hard. Everyone knew that this little girl was fighting for her life.

Ruby and Jack stood on the rooftop, watching as the team took charge, their own part in saving the child over. A sense of inadequacy touched Ruby even though she knew she'd done all she could and their patient was better off with the hospital team now. Glancing at Jack, she saw him swallow hard.

'You were awesome with her,' she said.

'Thanks, Red. It's never enough, though, is it?'

'Sometimes it has to be.' Unfortunately. The downside of the job.

Jack looked down into her eyes and for a moment they connected. Really hooked up. Ruby forgot to breathe. Forgot where she was. Forgot about the waiting 'copter. Only Jack mattered.

And how good it felt to be with him again. With Jack at her side she could accomplish anything. Even staying in Wellington for ever.

Behind her Chris called out to them, 'Time to hit the sky, you two.'

And Ruby leapt away. Jack wasn't by her side, figuratively or otherwise. And never would be. Racing for the 'copter, she chastised herself for her odd moment of wishful thinking. She wasn't the same person any more, and from what little she'd seen so far, neither was Jack. Getting together again would never work out. They hadn't managed to stay together when they'd been happy and in love. How could they possibly have a workable relationship with all that hurt they'd inflicted on each other?

CHAPTER THREE

AS THE helicopter settled on the hard back at base, Ruby glanced at her watch. Six forty-five. Yee-ha. She could sign off and go home. Grab some take-aways for her dinner on the way. Feed Zane. Put distance between her and Jack. Take time to absorb her initial impressions, think about the differences she'd already noted in him.

Up front Chris clicked off numerous switches as the whine of the rotors slowed. Then he poked his head around the bulkhead. 'Dave's just come through, says to meet him at the Aero House for beers. Something to do with you, Jack. An unofficial welcome aboard sort of thing.'

The Aero House was the local watering hole, frequented mostly by pilots and the girls hoping to nab them. The rescue staff used it regularly for winding down from bad days, for having a quiet drink with people who understood they didn't always want to talk about work, and occasionally for partying.

Jack said, 'Sounds good to me. Ruby?'

Going home where Jack wasn't in her face all the time, where she could breathe without effort, was her preferred option. But this was the team, her family of sorts and, whatever her feelings, Jack was being made a part of it. 'Sure, a cold one is just what I need.'

One beer and then she could leave guilt-free. Hopefully no one had a mind to start a party. Not on a Sunday night.

'Let's top up the packs and get out of here.' Jack dropped to the ground and reached up for the bags Ruby handed down.

She finished cleaning up inside the 'copter and dropped the dirty laundry bag outside for pick-up in the morning.

'Have a busy night.' Ruby waved goodbye to the night crews a little while later and headed out to the well-lit parking lot. As she tossed her bag into the cab of her truck she heard Jack say, 'What are you driving now?'

She grinned. 'Nothing like my old car, is it?'

And her grin widened at the stunned look on his face.

'You haven't borrowed it?' He stared at her shining black pride and joy. 'This truck's yours?'

'Right down to the last wheel nut. Isn't it fabulous?' She ran a hand over the bonnet. It still thrilled her to drive this beast. And she so loved the stares she got whenever she pulled into the yard at the building centre and clambered out.

'It's seen a few kilometres.' Jack nodded at a couple of minor dents.

Hello? A new one cost a fortune, and she certainly didn't have that sort of money lolling around in her bank account to spend on a vehicle. Not when her house was costing a bomb. 'I bought it privately for a bargain. My old neighbour's son was moving to Australia and wanted to get rid of it. He gave me a good deal if I promised to keep an eye out for his mother.' Funny how her luck had started to change from the day she'd decided to put the Greaser into perspective. The moment she'd let go all the anger at his betrayal of her and Mum, her life had begun looking up. A quick glance at Jack had her wondering just how high it could go.

Jack's eyes popped. 'You're kidding me?' But then he shook his head. 'No, not with that smug look on your face. And judging by the gleaming paint work, this is your most prized possession. It's fantastic. Way to go, Red.' Jack strolled around the truck, looking it over with something like envy in those gunmetal eyes.

She couldn't resist showing off her wagon. 'Can I give you a ride to the Aero House?'

'Thanks, but I'll see you there.' He waved the keys he held between thumb and forefinger towards a saloon, and the sound of locks popping was loud in the frosty air. 'I'll take the old dunger.'

'Want me to follow in case you break down?' she quipped.

'Lady, you might have the wheels but I've got the experience.'

'Is that a challenge?' The words were dry on her tongue. He'd always had way more experience than her at almost everything. Especially in bed. He'd been her first lover. The one-off couplings she'd tried in her rebellious teens didn't count.

'It would be if we had somewhere to race, and I

had time to put a V8 under the hood.' His hands were light on his slim hips, his gaze thoughtful. Then he shifted his hands to her shoulders and drew her nearer. 'How have you been, Red? Really?'

Swallow. Gulp. 'Um, good, great.' Duh. She shrugged from under his hands, certain she'd have more chance of stringing a sentence together if he wasn't touching her. 'And you?' she croaked.

'Me? A bunch of fluffy ducks.' His eyes didn't lighten up one bit. 'We'd better move it or the others will be wondering what's happened to us.'

And knowing those guys, they'd have no restraints about asking what she was doing chatting to Jack in the car park at night. She swung up into the cab and turned the motor over. Just one beer and then she'd head home to her little piece of paradise. Paradise without Jack? The picture was starting to look all wrong.

Jack watched in awe as tiny Red settled on cushions and stretched her legs towards the pedals. The big vehicle dwarfed her already short frame. Heck, she almost fell out reaching for the door to slam it shut. But as she pulled away she was sitting up straight, her arms out level as she gripped the steering-wheel, pride pushing her chin forward.

A warm sensation curled around his heart, and an involuntary smile tugged at his lips. She was still a spunky woman. She intrigued him, despite that screaming, bottled-red hair that had shocked him when he'd first seen her again. She seemed more relaxed about life than he'd ever known her. Hell, she even appeared genuinely happy. So unlike the Ruby he'd loved. The Ruby he hadn't been able to help.

Had he tried hard enough? He certainly hadn't fought to keep her by his side. Neither had he tried to come to any arrangement where they went to the States together. It had been downright lousy of him to let her face that trip alone, but he'd been too wrapped up in his own injured pride to look past her brave words and see what it was she'd really wanted. That had only become apparent as she'd slid away from him at the airport. Hunched in on herself, departure card, boarding pass and passport gripped in her white-knuckled hand, she'd ducked out of his life.

And now she was back.

Had things gone well with her father? For her sake he hoped so. She'd spent so long carrying that particular chip around it had soured her outlook on just about everything.

Gravel spat as she rolled quickly out onto the road. Jack grinned after her and headed for his wreck of a car. Too bad the mortgage hadn't allowed him to buy something bigger and better. The pay cut he'd taken to come here wouldn't help either but, according to his best mate who made truckloads on the fishing trawlers, money wasn't everything. But it sure helped.

The Aero House was quiet when he sat down, a beer in his hand, with his new workmates. Slats was not there, apparently not a very social man. Jack had automatically sought out the chair beside Ruby. Big mistake and too late to change. He wished he could ignore her, forget the past and all the great times they'd had together. He needed to focus on the future, the uncertainty of that still gnawing at his gut, keeping him awake at night wondering why he'd so impetuously walked away from the job he'd spent his adult life aiming for.

'So how did your first two trips go?' Dave asked from across the table.

Grateful for the interruption, Jack replied, 'Fairly good. I think.' He raised an eyebrow at Ruby, belatedly remembering she'd witnessed his moment of confusion before they'd landed at the site of the car accident. The last thing he wanted was for her to rat on him. But, then, he already knew she wouldn't. This reaction was all to do with how confused she made him feel around her. He needed to relax. Like, how?

'For a newbie you weren't bad.' She tipped her bottle to her lips and gave him a wink.

'Thanks a bundle,' he growled in mock seriousness. Then his gaze stuck on her throat as she swallowed. The warmth he'd felt in the car park became a raging inferno in his veins. So much for thinking of her as a teammate. Angry at himself for letting her get to him so easily, he jerked his head around, focused on the others at the table. His chair screeched on the floorboards as he put space between himself and Ruby. 'Yeah,' he drawled, 'I had a good afternoon.'

Except for having to pick up a little girl who might never get to go to school again, or play with her pals or even know what was going on around her. He'd give the hospital a call later on to see if there was any improvement. One of the advantages of having worked there was that someone would tell him what he wanted to know. Heaven help the girl's parents. Jack knew the horror and fear they'd be feeling. He'd seen that expression on his dad's face when he was seven, and even at that age it had been something he'd understood. And never forgotten.

Dave was talking to him. 'You'll soon have the hang of it. Anyway, we've got time to iron out anything you're not sure of.' Dave's leave didn't start until the following week. 'Here comes the other day crew. And Sandra.'

Jack was soon shaking hands all round and putting faces to names he'd read on the staff list. The tension that had niggled him all afternoon relaxed. Ruby, now slightly turned away from him, was talking to Sandra, one of the base's aeronautical engineers and apparently Chris's partner. Was Ruby avoiding him? Why would she? So far she'd treated him the same as the others. As he should be treating her. He was just being super-sensitive. He and Ruby were to be mates, and she was playing the game. What if he took her out for a meal so they could talk over things and definitely cement their new footing? Yeah, he liked that idea. But he'd wait for a quiet moment to ask her. It wouldn't do for the others to think he was favouring one of the team even if he hadn't officially started yet. And if he believed that then he was an even bigger fool than he already thought.

Half an hour later Derek, a paramedic on the second crew, stood up and said, 'Sorry, guys, but I promised the wife I wouldn't be too late tonight.'

Ruby drained her bottle. 'Me too. Not that I promised the wife anything, but Zane will be hanging out for his dinner. Jack, it's great to have you with us. Enjoy your days off, guys.'

'Thanks.' Zane? Who the hell was Zane? Acute disappointment rocked through Jack, tightened his gut. Come on. Even though he'd half expected her to have a boyfriend, finding out for sure didn't make him at all happy. Zane. What sort of moniker was that? Some American name?

Damn it, this is not how friends thought about each other. Jack shuddered. At least he'd saved himself from looking an idiot by asking her out for dinner.

Just then Chris returned from the bar with more beers. 'You still okay for me to take out those cupboards tomorrow morning, Ruby?'

'Looking forward to it.' She grinned, pushing back her chair.

'You don't get to swing that sledgehammer this time. I want the cupboards whole so I can sell them for you.' Chris sat and draped an arm around Sandra's shoulders. 'You okay with me spending a few hours at Ruby's?'

'I'll only be getting in the groceries so go for it,' Sandra replied. Then she nudged him in the ribs with an elbow. 'Gives me some time at home to myself.'

'Like I'm a proper pest.' Chris grinned.

Dave asked, 'Need a hand with those cupboards, Chris? I'm free until after lunch.'

'The more help the sooner we're done. It's not like little Ruby can hold the cupboards while I take them down.' Chris ducked as Ruby waved her empty bottle threateningly at him. 'Down, girl.'

Jack opened his mouth without thought. 'If it's more help you need, count me in.'

'Aren't you officially starting work tomorrow?' Ruby's eyes widened.

'Since Dave's off until Wednesday, we decided I'd start then,' Jack explained. Then, ignoring that 'don't come near' sign in her eyes, he asked, 'What's your address?'

Noting down her directions, a little devil stomped on his brain: bad move. Bad move. He had four months working with Red before he headed off on his next adventure far away from Wellington. Away from Ruby. He could do it. So why the feeling of standing on a precipice? Why the sudden urge to haul her into his arms and kiss her senseless? The answer blinded him. Because he wanted to go back to where they'd left off three years ago, to pick up their life and live through those missing years, that turmoil, and arrive here, today, together. Happy.

Ruby pushed her gate shut the next morning and unhitched Zane's lead. 'There you go, my boy. That walk should keep you happy for a few hours.'

She glanced up the path, looking to see if any of the guys had arrived yet. 'All quiet, Zany.'

Then she rounded the corner of her house and walked slap bang into someone. A man, if that hard body was anything to go by. 'Oof. Ouch. Sorry.'

Firm hands grabbed her shoulders, steadied her. 'Look where you're going, Red.'

What she looked at was the expanse of jersey-covered chest right in front of her eyes. All she breathed was that pine scent she'd smelt the day before. All her mind had in it was confusion. Heat seared her, pooled in her belly.

Jerking out of his hold, she glared up at him. 'What are you doing back here?'

'Looking for you. I forgot to ask what time the other guys were turning up so thought I'd better get here. Seems I'm early.'

'Chris won't be far away.' She hoped. Time alone with Jack was the last thing she needed. It made keeping the 'mates' thing too difficult. 'Let's have a coffee while we wait.' And she could put some space between them. Through the long, sleepless night she'd begun asking herself why Jack had never quite disappeared out of her heart, still lurked in the corners of her mind at the most unexpected moments. No matter how hard she'd tried to pretend he no longer mattered, it was now blatantly obvious to her that he did. She should send him packing before she got in too deep, before it became impossible to say goodbye again.

Before she hurt him once more. She'd do anything not to hurt Jack. Even leave Wellington? Put her own needs aside? Unlike last time. Maybe this was how she could make it up to him. But to let go of her dream, say goodbye to her roots and go. Go where? There was nowhere else she wanted to be, nowhere else she belonged—with or without Jack.

Peering up into those disturbing grey eyes, she couldn't think of anything to say without spilling her guts. 'Come inside,' she muttered.

'Some house you've got here. Love the land. I'm surprised no one thought to subdivide it. The grounds must keep you busy with mowing, pruning all those fruit trees and keeping that hedge in shape. What's the dark patch over there by the back fence?'

Glad to be on safe ground, she spewed out

words. 'Lupin. I'm wintering over the soil and come spring I'll plant my vegetable patch. Just think; fresh tomatoes, peas, lettuces, zucchinis, all at the end of the section.' Even she could manage making salads.

'I didn't think you knew what a spade was for.' Jack's face was neutral as he added in a flat voice, 'This speaks of permanence, Red.'

Red. All over her body her cells danced as his name for her tripped off his tongue. Red was that woman from a long time ago. That woman he'd made love to, tenderly, feverishly, exquisitely, often. Every time he called her Red she wanted to strip down naked and pole dance for him. Which would shock the hell out of her workmates if they arrived midway through.

But to answer his underlying criticism. 'I didn't buy the house on a whim, Jack. I want somewhere I can call home, for ever.' That should knock his socks off.

Those thick, dark eyebrows rose in a disconcerting fashion. 'You've been here how long? Two months?' The sarcasm dripped off his tongue like lemon juice.

'Long enough to know I've bought the perfect

property for me. It's where I want to put down roots, and not just the plant kind.' Dredging up a smile, she hooked her shoes off. She would not let him get to her, wouldn't let him undermine her resolve. She could do that all by herself. 'I'll be like that walnut tree out there, here for decades.'

He stared at the gnarled tree she nodded at for a moment, then turned his gaze to the exterior of the house. 'I'd have thought you'd want modern. All these weatherboards need regular upkeep. A lot of commitment goes with a place like this.'

'Commitment I'm learning to make.' She widened her smile especially for Jack, swallowed her despair at his disbelief. 'This is a long-term project. And I love the character that comes with old homes. Far more interesting and less predictable.'

The tone of his voice matched the scepticism darkening his eyes, but he did ask, 'Do I get a guided tour?'

'Later.' They'd start with the kitchen and that drink. Hopefully the others would arrive before she had time to show him anything else. Somewhere deep inside she felt a twist of reluctance, as though by opening up her home to him she'd be exposing her soul and showing him a side of herself he'd never seen. How could he have? She'd not long found it herself. So what was she afraid of? That he'd take fright? Run away? This was all so, so damned hard.

She stepped past him and tripped over her dog. 'Zane, out of the way. Oh, no, naughty boy.' Ruby grabbed Zane's collar and hauled him away from Jack's bootlaces.

Jack blinked, gaping at her black Labrador. 'That's Zane?'

She squinted at Jack, then Zane. Nodding. 'Yes, this is my dog.' Who else could Zane be? He'd thought Zane was her man. She chuckled. It was true. Zane guarded her, protected her, played with her and gave her loads of love. The perfect male, actually.

Jack's face flushed a delicious red. 'How long have you had him?'

'I got him from the SPCA seven weeks ago. He'd been dumped as a six-month-old pup and no one wanted him because he's blind in one eye from being poked with a stick. The moment I saw Zane I had to have him. When I knelt down to pet this guy through the wire of his cage, he licked me and I was a goner.'

'Blimey, you're becoming a right softie, as well as very domesticated.' Jack peered down at her, amusement mixed with confusion colouring those steely eyes. 'House. Dog. Truck. What's next?'

'Nothing I can think of.' Except a hot man to come home to at the end of every shift. Pity the one she was thinking of obviously didn't think she had stickability, so there went that idea. Not that it had had any substance in the first place. They'd done their time together, and now they were meant to have moved on. Great theory. A shame it wasn't ringing true for her. A sigh trickled past her lips and she changed the subject to a safer topic. 'I'm sorry Zane's undone your laces but be glad he hasn't had time to eat them. Laces are his favourite distraction at the moment. Last week it was underwear.' Gulp. Shouldn't have said that.

'Underwear?' His eyes suddenly twinkled wickedly. A crooked grin split his face, and set butterflies flapping in her tummy. 'Yours, I take it.'

She sucked chilly air through clenched teeth. 'Sometimes but not always. Old Mrs Crocombe next door lost a pair of bloomers off her clothes horse last week.' A giggle erupted up her throat as a picture rose in her mind. 'Zane looked hilarious with them draped over his head. Thankfully Mrs Crocombe thought so too.'

'I thought bloomers went out with my great-grandmother.' Jack shook his head as he retied his laces. 'Seriously, does your neighbour really wear them?'

'Big pink ones. With wide elastic around the legs that caught in Zane's eye teeth.' Another giggle broke through. 'She's ninety-two not out.'

'Ahh, the neighbour you're keeping a watch over.' Jack rubbed Zane's ears. 'Where'd your name come from, dog?'

Zane licked Jack's hand as Ruby answered. 'They gave him that at the SPCA. Zane for zany. It suits him.'

'What will you do with him when you leave Wellington again?'

She snapped, 'Zane will long have been resting under the walnut tree by the time I even consider moving away.' Ruby crossed her fingers and headed inside. 'Give me a break, Jack.' Was it that she'd chosen this particular city that stuck in his craw? Did he think she'd invaded his territory? He only had himself to blame for that. This was the place she'd been happiest, the one town she'd struggled to leave. Because of Jack.

Jack straightened up and rubbed his gritty eyes. Sleep had been elusive last night as his mind had chased images of Ruby. The old Ruby struggling to become a nurse. Paramedic Ruby performing highly competently yesterday with her patients. Both versions had tangled and twined in his brain, giving him a headache. He had to keep reminding himself there was only one Ruby. One he couldn't rely on for any sort of permanence. Not that he would be going down that path with her again.

He followed her inside. He'd work on the presumption that deep down Ruby was still Ruby, and that well within twelve months she'd be casting around for a new city to try out. That way he'd survive the turmoil rolling through him when he was with her, when he thought of her in the middle of the night, when he heard her sweet laughter around the base. That way he'd remember to keep everything on a friendship level. That way he wouldn't risk being left again.

Ever since yesterday that prickly, restless feeling that had driven him to quit the hospital and take on the rescue job had started begging to be scratched again. He'd believed he'd doused the itch by getting different, exciting work outside his normal sphere of comfort. He was on the move himself these days. Rescue helicopters, the deep south, then who knew where? Yet, in one emotion-packed moment of reunion, he was wondering what his life was really all about.

Had he got it wrong leaving the A and E department? He'd loved his job—the work, staff, patients who needed his skills. But something had been missing. Something that had started small and grown bigger with each passing week until he'd snapped. Gone and got a temporary job. Given up his awesome career. For what? He wasn't sure now.

In her cramped kitchen he looked around, trying to keep a space between him and Ruby. Hard to do when the room was the size of a toy box. Sucking in a Ruby-scented breath, he asked, 'Have you got flatmates?'

'Not yet. I thought about it but no one in their right mind would want to live here when I'm busy pulling the house to bits.' Flicking on the tap to fill the kettle, she asked, 'What about you? Are you sharing a place with someone?'

Was she asking if he lived with someone special? 'I bought a four-year-old house in partnership with Steve and Johnny. Neither of them is home much so they've got a base to return to whenever they want. And it makes good financial sense to share the mortgage while we're all doing other things with our incomes.' He chuckled. 'Actually, the house is only about three kilometres from here on the other side of Mount Vic.'

Ruby nibbled her bottom lip. 'Sounds a perfect solution for all of you. So if Steve's flying 747s, is he an international pilot now? He must be stoked. That has always been his goal.'

'He's based in Dubai but heads home for a few days every second month.' His brother needed to keep those family ties alive to stay on an even keel in his chaotic, globetrotting life. Truthfully Jack needed Steve to need him. It was a lifetime habit that had kept him sane and safe and he wasn't about to break it. At a very young age Jack had deliberately made himself the centre of the universe for his dad and Steve. That way they'd never leave him as Mum and Beth had. At seven it had all made perfect sense. At thirty he saw no reason to change.

He continued, 'Johnny works long and hard as a skipper on a fishing trawler, saving every cent for the day when he can buy his own boat.' The perfect flatmates, hardly ever there but when they were they were great for parties and going to the odd rugby match.

'Remember that horrible old flat we shared with Tina and Gerry? Cold and dark in winter, hot and stuffy in summer. And the neighbour was so noisy you used earplugs so you could get some sleep.' Ruby shuddered. 'And yet I loved it at the time.'

'It was very handy for Courtney Place and all the pubs and cafés. If I remember correctly we spent most of our spare time down there playing pool and drinking beer.' Jack looked wistful for a moment. Then he pulled a chair out from the table and straddled it.

'The whole flat wasn't much bigger than this tiny kitchen.' Nostalgia filled Ruby's eyes. 'We were happy there.'

Jack gasped at the intensity in her voice. Red

was right. They had been very happy. 'We didn't need much to get by on back then.'

'Just as well. Nowhere to store anything. You ever hear from Tina and Gerry?'

Jack shook his head. More people who'd moved out of his life. 'They're in Dunedin now. Gerry's a GP and Tina's got her own interior design shop.'

'I wonder if Tina ever made up with her sister after that horrendous argument over where to scatter their father's ashes.' Ruby tapped her mouth. 'Families, eh? They certainly put people through a lot.'

And now Ruby didn't have one. At least, not here in New Zealand. Jack missed his chance to ask about her father when she said, 'At least with Zane I know exactly where I stand. Chief provider of life's essentials in return for complete loyalty and undivided love.' She stared at her mutt with an odd blend of love and sadness in her eyes.

Was that where *he* had failed her? By not providing those things? He had loved her. He had been loyal. To the point where Ruby had come first? No. Definitely not.

'So how do you think we're going to go, working together?' Ruby banged two cups on the stainless-steel bench.

Stunned at the sudden change of subject, he muttered, 'Can't see why it won't be okay.'

She leaned back against the bench. 'It has to be unless you want to change your mind about continuing at Rescue.' She lifted one eyebrow at him. 'Because I have no intention of leaving.'

He swallowed a retort. 'It won't come to that, Red.'

'I'm Ruby. Think you can remember that? Ruby.' Worry flittered through her eyes. She looked uneasy. Because of him? Did he still un-nerve her? Male pride puffed out his chest. He liked it that he'd had some effect on her. But his pride quickly deflated. Ruby was right to worry. They were supposed to be mates, not ex-lovers looking for a road back to each other's arms. Damn it, because right now the thought of being held by Red was the most attractive notion he could come up with.

'Believe it or not, I'm trying. But old habits tend to hang around.' He stared at her, her trou-bled eyes disconcerting him. 'Ruby.'

The sound of a heavy toolbag being dropped

onto the back porch saved him from unwisely delving any deeper into whatever was bothering her. He didn't want to know, didn't need to get involved. She was sorting out her life—he had his own to think about.

Chris called out, 'Hey, hope you've got the kettle on. It's frigid out here.'

'Dave with you?' Ruby called back.

'Yep, he's bringing in the crowbars. Jack here already?'

'Yes.' Jack shuffled around to make room for the two men, bumped into Red. Catching his breath, he carefully eased sideways from her soft, pliant body. 'How are we all going to squeeze in here and bring those cupboards down?' Couldn't Ruby go to town or anywhere far away from him?

'We'll manage,' Chris told him.

Ruby spooned coffee granules into two more mugs, shovelled sugar on top. 'Let's drink up and get cracking.'

Jack couldn't agree more. The sooner they started the sooner they'd be done.

But a little while later Chris swore out loud and then said, 'Cupboards aren't coming down as easily as they should. We mightn't be able to save them after all, Ruby.'

Her hands slapped onto her hips as she glared at the offending cupboards. 'If you can't, then you can't.' She craned her neck and peered up into a corner where Chris had prised off some timber. 'What's through that gap? It's like another ceiling.'

Chris slid the ladder across and climbed up, poked a crowbar through where Ruby indicated. 'Great. Fantastic. Just what you don't need. I'd say that's the original ceiling and this one...' he tapped above his head '...is a false one.'

'Another darned complication.' Ruby's brow crinkled as she continued to stare upwards, blinking rapidly.

'I should've expected it. False ceilings are common in older houses where the original ones are very high. People renovate, putting in new, lower ceilings to help keep rooms warm.' Chris dropped to the floor. 'Ruby, you'd better put your kitchen designer on hold until we're done with hauling out these cupboards and I can ascertain just what's up there. You might want to pull out the false ceiling.'

'That'd mean a lot more cabinetry, wouldn't it? I couldn't have a gap above the new cupboards. It would look odd.' Ruby's teeth nibbled her bottom lip, worry clouding her eyes.

Jack somehow refrained from giving her a hug, those imminent tears piercing his heart. 'Sounds expensive.' Ruby wouldn't be able to afford big changes, surely?

Chris picked up the jemmy again. 'You still happy to carry on, even if I have to wreck them, Ruby?'

Her sigh filled the room. 'Definitely. They've got to go, they're far too ugly.' She shook her head. 'Nothing's ever straightforward, is it?'

Not with Red, that was for sure. Jack picked up a second crowbar and joined Chris. 'What do you want me to do?'

Ruby watched every move the men made. Every screech as a nail was ripped out underlined her fear of not being able to complete her plans for her future. Her whole life plan started here. If this went wrong, so might everything else, eventually driving her away. Her heart blocked her throat. Chris had warned her old houses held secrets, secrets that would have an impact on her bank account. She had a reasonable-sized budget but too many added expenses might jeopardise everything.

It was one o'clock before the walls were clear, and the false ceiling completely exposed. Ruby turned to Dave. 'Thank you so much. I'll rustle up some lunch for you all.'

Dave chuckled. 'Don't bother for me, Ruby. I'm not hungry.' Then he called to Chris and Jack, who were wrestling an undamaged cupboard through the back door onto the porch, 'Ruby's keen to make you some lunch. That okay?'

Chris stopped moving, a grin on his face. 'Not for me, thanks. I'm thinking of my stomach.'

Ruby reached for the phone and began punching in a familiar number. 'So I'll order pizza for one, shall I?'

'Ha, ha, very funny.' Chris stepped backwards and Jack at last could put down his end of the cupboard.

'Are these things lead lined, or what?' He straightened his back with a groan. From inside he heard Ruby order three pizzas. 'What's with the lunch?'

'Ruby's not the best cook on the block. Last

time she rustled up something we all had a guts ache for hours.'

Had Ruby done much cooking when they'd been together? Nothing came to Jack's mind except two-minute noodles and instant-soup packets. But the four of them sharing the flat had always been too busy to do anything more strenuous than grab 'heat and eat' food. At last, something about her that hadn't changed. He smiled as warmth touched his bones and charged his hormones.

Ruby was back in town.

And in a short while he'd be leaving. He'd finally learned his lessons from those he loved. His sister and mother. Gone. His father and brother. Moved elsewhere. Ruby. Gone. Now back. But not for long. Despite all her assurances. He knew her too well to believe a word of them.

CHAPTER FOUR

'WHAT'S next on your list of things to do here?' Dave asked Ruby as they devoured the welcome pizzas.

'I've got to get that old vinyl off the kitchen floor before the new units go in, even if I do change the plans. The floor-sander guy said he'd be here next Monday.' Ruby licked a thread of cheese off her chin and pretended Jack wasn't watching. 'That job should keep me busy for the rest of my days off.' For the next month more like. It was hard work, scraping the well-glued floor-covering off with a spade. But when the kauri boards beneath were sanded and polished the result would be worth every drop of sweat. As long there weren't any nasty surprises beneath the vinyl.

Jack's eyes were still fixed on her chin. 'Want a hand? I'm not doing anything this afternoon.'

Like she was going to turn down an offer like

that. Even from Jack. 'I'll order in more pizzas for dinner.'

'I take it that's a yes,' Jack said, with more force than needed. Regretting his offer already?

'You're a sucker for punishment.' Dave punched him lightly on the biceps. 'Ruby's a slave-driver.'

'Thanks, Dave. Go ahead and scare my worker away.' Ruby gathered up empty pizza boxes and slid past Jack, careful not to touch him and yet still her shoulder brushed his chest. She stumbled. Righted herself. Headed out to the rubbish bin and squashed the boxes on top of previous take-out containers.

She could hear Chris saying, 'This house is going to be spectacular when Ruby's done.' Her heart swelled with pride.

'It must be costing a bundle.' Jack's low voice held a question.

He didn't know about the money she'd inherited from her mother. An amount big enough to make this house a tribute to her mum. It was her way of expressing her deep sorrow for all the pain she'd caused while growing up. She shuddered as a chill slid across her skin. If only there was a way to take back the terrible things she'd said whenever they'd talked about the Greaser. Ruby had blamed her mother for wrecking her life by keeping her father's whereabouts a secret when all along her mother had been protecting her.

'That's why I hope to sell those cupboards for Ruby,' Chris, who knew nothing about her inheritance either, told Jack. 'Every dollar counts.'

As Ruby sauntered inside, Chris hoisted his toolbag and strode to the door. 'See you Wednesday, Ruby, Jack. You want a lift somewhere, Dave?'

'Chris makes me sound like a charity case.' Ruby stared through the window, watching her friends tramping down the path.

Jack leaned against the bench. 'You're lucky to have their help.'

'I helped paint the inside of Chris and Sandra's house the first weeks I was here.'

'I'm not criticising, Red. It's wonderful that you all get on so well. And from what I've seen, it reflects in your work at the base. We never had anything like that at A and E.' Without the cupboards to absorb sound his words echoed quietly around them, creating a cosy feeling.

'Why did you change jobs? I thought you'd be

there for a few years once you were made Head of Department. That was your plan.' That was why it had been pointless to wait until he qualified before she went to the States. Seems she'd got it wrong.

She moved to fill the kettle. Something to occupy her hands. From somewhere deep inside her soul came a fierce urge to reach out to Jack, to slip her arms around his waist and touch those full lips with hers. The kettle overflowed. Snapping the tap off, she thumped the jug on the bench.

Despite the increased kitchen space with the cupboards gone, the room was far too small for both of them. Goose-bumps rose on her arms when Jack looked at her.

'You knew I'd made HOD?'

Huh? What did that have to do with anything? Concentrate. 'I'm sorry, I only found out when you got the job working with us. I knew how much you'd wanted it so it surprised me to find you'd given it up.' Regret singed her. She'd deliberately not kept up to date with what Jack had been doing. It would've only made her even more unhappy. Now a trillion questions flicked up in her mind about what he'd been doing since she'd left town.

His lips flattened as he stared thoughtfully at his feet for a few minutes. Finally he said, 'It was the job I'd wanted since the day I decided to specialise in emergency medicine, and when I was offered the position I felt everything I'd worked so hard for had come together.'

'So why the sadness?' The question was out before she thought about the sanity of getting involved in something so personal with him.

'Sad? Me? I don't think so.'

Ruby did, but she refrained from pressing further. 'So why leave?'

'I wanted to try other jobs that my qualifications lend themselves to.'

Ruby jerked her chin up. 'So what have you got planned after the Rescue job?'

'I've applied to go to Scott Base for the summer.'

Ruby felt her jaw drop. 'What?' This was so unlike Jack. Changing careers in midstream was surprising enough, but going to Antarctica? Growing a tail would seem more feasible. What had happened to make him seek a different career? Jack had had to struggle to pay his way through med school so he probably still required the fat pay packet that came with being Head of Department.

'There's more to life than being tied up running a busy emergency department.'

Ruby's jaw cracked as it dropped further. 'So you're looking for some excitement?'

Jack grinned that heart-stopping grin. 'What's wrong with that? Wanting some fun? It's not as though I've spent a lot of time doing anything other than studying and working. Didn't you join for the exhilaration of jumping out of helicopters?'

She shuddered exaggeratedly. 'Hardly. I loved the pace of ambulance work and hadn't intended giving it up. Being on the trucks, out there amongst it, looking out for people made me feel I was doing some good.'

'Sounds like excitement to me. And it's not as though having fun while doing your job brings the standard of care down.'

'I guess, but I never looked at it like that. I turned down my first opportunity to work on the helicopters in San Francisco. Me leap out of a flying machine? That wasn't exciting, that was downright scary.' Ruby sighed, dredged up a smile. 'I got conned into going for a ride, and from then on I was hooked. Literally. The guys had me strapped and latched and swinging over a field in no time at all. I loved it.'

'I know what you mean. But it's still emergency medicine, right at the edge.'

'It is, but mostly it's about helping people when they're facing their worst nightmare.' About caring, about saving lives. This was getting too deep with a man she didn't want to do deep with yet. Liar. Wasn't that what she really wanted? To get to know Jack all over again?

Again? They hadn't known each other very well last time. Now she was beginning to understand that they'd shared only the fun times. There'd been no discussions about what they'd wanted for the future. They hadn't even known each other's tastes in houses. She loved old, he obviously liked modern. On the other hand, they were both dedicated to helping people. She waved a teaspoon at him. 'You want another coffee before we start on this floor?'

'Please. I'll just make a call.'

Ruby stirred the coffee then headed out into the chilly air, Zane at her heels. She rubbed his ears. 'It's not walk time yet. Give me a couple of hours attacking that damned vinyl and then we'll negotiate terms.'

Zane ran past her to the base of a tree and snapped up a tennis ball, racing back to drop it at Ruby's feet.

'Didn't you hear a word I said?' She tossed the ball at the solid wooden fence. Zane sped across the wet, slippery lawn, snatching at his toy and missing, finally picking it up and returning to her.

After the fifth toss Ruby laughed. 'That's it for now. I've got work to do.'

'He's full of energy, isn't he?' Jack said from behind her, causing her to nearly leap out of her skin. 'Here, Zane, I'll throw that for you.'

Zane obliged, not at all fazed over who played with him, just so long as someone did.

'He's getting better at retrieving the ball. Sometimes I think he uses his blind eye.' Ruby went to collect the spades and some cartons to put the vinyl in and headed back to the house, Jack and Zane following.

Jack told her, 'I checked with the hospital. There's no change with Lily Byrne. She's still in an induced coma.'

The little girl they'd lifted from the car crash yesterday. The downside to their job. A long, slow breath slid out of one corner of Ruby's mouth. 'Those poor parents. They must be going through hell. I really hope Lily comes right. She's so young.'

'Unimaginable what her folks must be feeling.'

Something in Jack's voice made her study him closely. 'You had a moment there yesterday when we first heard about Lily.'

'Yeah, I did.' He lifted one of the spades and began scraping at the floor. Immediately the spade edge snagged and skidded across the vinyl. 'Our sister died of head injuries when she was four. Every time I have to attend a child with those types of injuries I have a moment, as you call it.'

'You had a sister?' She reached a hand to him. 'Jack, I didn't know.' *You never told me. What other important things did you avoid mentioning?*

He twisted away, putting space between them. 'I don't talk about her.'

'Obviously.' He couldn't have hurt her more if he'd tried, turning from her like that. Swallowing hard, she focused on her coffee. Ready with a hug if he needed one. Would he tell her more?

Finally he continued, 'I remember the expression on Dad's face as if it was yesterday. That look of terror has stayed with me all my life. The awful fear, the complete helplessness of the situation, waiting for someone to fix his child. When they couldn't, when she died, Dad just—just crumbled.'

Ruby couldn't wait any longer to be asked. He might never get around to it. She tried not to think how he'd just revealed more about his past than he'd done in all the time they'd been together before. Instead, she stepped close and wrapped her arms around him. Held him tight. Giving him the only thing she had to offer. Felt free to offer. In any capacity he chose to accept.

Jack froze, his back rigid under her hands. Ruby held him, saying nothing, her fingers making soothing circles, her palms pressing into him. Slowly, slowly, he began relaxing. His arms slid around her back. Did he even know he was pulling her ever so slightly closer? Time to shift away, before this got too involved, too awkward. But her legs wouldn't move, had turned bone-less. Instead, her arms tightened further. Here in Jack's embrace was where she belonged. This was what she'd been hankering after for three long, lonely years. Why she'd come home.

That didn't make any of this right. If they were to get back together there was a lot to discuss first, issues to clear up. She began to tug back, common sense starting to prevail. She couldn't, shouldn't, revisit the past. She'd hurt Jack, and herself, by leaving. She didn't deserve a second chance.

Jack's hands slid over her back, a caressing movement that stole the air out of her lungs, nul-lified the common sense trying to take hold of her mind. When he wrapped his hands over her shoulders and tipped her slightly backwards she knew he was going to kiss her and she was pow-erless to stop him. She wanted it. Forget right or wrong. This was Jack and she was finally kiss-ing him. Common sense was highly overrated.

His mouth touched hers; softly, tentatively. Seeking what? A connection from the past? A new beginning? She thrilled as his lips moulded with hers. And when she opened her mouth under his, her tongue tasted him. And Jack went from slow and quiet to fast and hot in an instant. His kiss deepened so quickly Ruby was spinning through space. Her arms gripped him tighter for support, trying to keep her firmly in the here and now as she tilted further back to allow Jack better access to her mouth.

At last. She was kissing Jack Forbes again. Memories of other kisses flooded her senses. Nothing over those years had changed. They fitted together. They were two halves that needed their matching piece to be complete. And yet this kiss felt different from every other kiss she'd shared with Jack. Filled with need so long held in abeyance. Filled with promise of new beginnings.

Heat zinged along her veins, dipped through her body, lit the dampened fires of desire she'd been denying since setting eyes on Jack close up yesterday. No other man had ever made her feel so weak, so tight, so warm, so needy, all in an instant. Just by kissing her, Jack turned on every switch her body had.

He walked her backwards up to the wall, his mouth not breaking contact with hers for a moment. Pressed against the wall, Ruby wriggled up onto her toes, all the better to continue kissing him. And as she did, she rubbed against his arousal, turning her heat into a conflagration. They were going to make love. The need, the desire, pulsed between them, hummed in her blood, tasted sweet in Jack's mouth.

Then Jack lifted his head and hurriedly stepped back. Ruby stumbled, steadied herself. 'Jack?'

His gaze was dark, deep. Wariness slowly filtered through the desire, cooling it. Caution took over and he stepped further away, taking his warm hands from her shoulders. 'Sorry.'

'You're sorry?' Pain sliced at her. He'd rejected her. Then anger emerged within her, drowning out the hurt he'd inflicted. Because Jack wanted her. He couldn't hide that. Desire had turned his eyes smoky, made his hands warm on her skin. What about his hard need that had pressed against her belly? He wanted her. Why had he broken off?

'Yes, I am.' Dragging a hand over his dark hair he winced. 'Very sorry.'

He sounded like he meant it. The pizza in her belly soured and she swallowed an acid lump in her throat. 'Sorry why, Jack? Because we kissed? Or is there another reason? Another woman?' She paused, remembering the blonde she'd seen him with.

He shook his head, not really an answer. But if there had been someone else, he'd never have kissed her.

She added, 'I'll tell you this for nothing. I don't regret you kissing me. Or that I kissed you back.' But did he have to kiss like the devil and then expect her to be happy when he stopped? At least she knew where she stood with him. They wouldn't be having an affair, not even a brief one. They couldn't even manage the friends thing yet. Her heart rolled over painfully. Talk about stupid. Why had she let him kiss her? Deep down she'd known kissing with Jack had to be avoided at all costs.

She should be grateful one of them had had the strength to haul on the brakes before they'd gone further and headed down the hall to her bedroom. Hadn't she earlier decided to get to know Jack properly this time? Whatever they'd started today had to end now.

Jack spun around and stared out the window.

His shoulders dropped as he rammed his hands into his jeans pockets. The silence between them stretched out, growing chillier as the seconds ticked by. Finally, when she couldn't stand it another moment, he turned back.

Anger spat out at her from those steely eyes. 'Why didn't you look me up when you first got back?'

She gasped. 'I did.' Once.

'Yeah, right. Was I asleep? Did I miss something?'

You were out with the blonde sticking plaster, having a lovey-dovey moment in the café at the end of your road. 'No one answered the doorbell so you might've been asleep.'

'You didn't think to come back another time?'

And get to meet Blondie face to face? 'I *have* been busy. I haven't got around to looking up anyone from the old days yet.'

'I deserve better than that. I wasn't just anyone.' He stamped across the room, reached the door and yanked it open. 'Let's stick to professional and friendly. Nothing more. Nothing less. What happened a moment ago will not happen again. Got it?'

'Loud and clear.' She was sorry she'd hurt him, very sorry. But her one attempt to see him had underlined the fact that she couldn't waltz back into his life and pick up where she'd left off. Straightening her spine, tugging her chin up, she locked eyes with him. 'I'll see you at work and not before.'

Then she picked up the spade and began to attack the vinyl with renewed vigour. Slam. A piece the size of a fifty-cent coin flicked through the air and hit the wall. Slam. Another piece spun off.

Jack watched her from the door. Please go, she begged silently. She was starting to feel like an idiot. Cold, hard reality had a certain chill to it. They had made a mistake. She glared at him. 'For the record, you're right. We need to keep our relationship light and friendly.' Not intense and sexual.

His beautiful mouth tightened. 'I'm glad you see things my way.'

His way? 'Don't get me started.' Another piece of vinyl spun across the floor. His way?

Everything had been going perfectly until Jack had stepped back into her life. The plans for her kitchen, her job. Even her lack of a love life hadn't bothered her. Now? Now she had more problems than she knew what to do with.

Jack braked sharply at the bottom of the hill. Fleeing from Ruby. Now, there was a laugh. Hilarious—not. A total role reversal. That mind-blowing kiss stayed with him, making his heated blood race. Pressing his foot harder on the accelerator, he careered out onto the main road. It seemed he couldn't leave the heady taste of Ruby behind. Not even her lack of a real answer about looking him up dampened the fires raging through his body. Another woman? Where did Ruby get such a notion?

There'd been huge disappointment in her jade eyes when he'd stopped kissing her.

What about *his* disappointment? He still didn't know how he'd managed to drag his mouth away from those lips that tasted of nectar. He'd wanted—needed—to take her there and then. The tension had been building all morning. Yet somehow reality had turned a cog, clicked some sense into his brain. At least he wouldn't be lead-ing Ruby on only to desert her in a few months' time. She could be grateful for that.

In self-defence he'd got angry with her. And she'd got angry back. At last the Ruby he recognised. A quick burst of temper had always been her way of getting out of a tight spot.

And sometimes her anger wasn't a quick burst. More like a hard, slow burn that she'd still hold a week from now. And behind that burn was a big glob of hurt. He'd rejected her. And she hated that. She could reject him, but take it in return? Not at all.

Right now relief should be pouring through him that he'd got away before going too far. It was Ruby's fault they'd kissed. She was too attractive. Temptation in a small, neat body that made him forget his hurt at her not calling in to see him since she'd returned. So he should slow down and relax, put out of his head the feeling of her lips on his. His hormones could go back into hibernation instead of overheating his body.

Toot, toot. A car cut him off, the driver waving a fist at him.

'What did I do?' Jack glanced in the rear-view mirror, side mirrors, couldn't see anything out of order. He checked the speedo. 'Yikes. Now I'm crawling along like I've got four flats.'

He indicated to pull over and slipped into a parking space right beside the beach. A brisk walk would help clear his head of all things Ruby.

His cellphone rang. Snatching it up from the passenger seat, he paused to check who was calling. If it was Ruby he'd ignore her. Really? Fortunately he didn't have to make that decision. 'Hey, Tony, how's things?'

His flying instructor replied, 'I've had a cancellation. You want to go for a buzz around the sky? Practise those engine-failure procedures?'

'Yes.' Jack tapped his fist on the steering-wheel. 'Yes.' An answer from heaven. Concentrating on putting his plane down in a tiny paddock without actually landing would send images of Ruby to Arizona. 'Give me fifteen. I'll drop in at home and grab my logbook.'

Jack didn't think of Ruby for thirty-two minutes, the whole time he was piloting the two-seater airplane.

But as he shoved the plane's door wide to step down onto the strut she reappeared, banging around inside his skull. Those piercing green eyes accused him of letting her down by stopping that kiss. The way she'd attacked the floor like her life had depended on it. The floor he'd offered to help with clearing, and which would take her twice as long to finish now that he'd stormed out. A sneaky feeling of guilt shimmied through him. It was easy to blame Ruby for everything. She'd done the leaving but not once had he offered to put his life on hold to go with her. Impractical for sure, but it might've been the right thing to do. Given the same circumstances, would he go now? He squashed that question firmly into the too-hard basket.

It was Zane who noticed him first. 'Hey, dog, how's your mum? Calmed down a bit?'

'That depends why you've come back.' Ruby stood on the porch, another coffee mug clasped in her hands, Zane's ball at her feet.

He was there because he had to prove their kiss had meant absolutely nothing. 'Figured you still needed a hand with that vinyl despite what went down between us earlier.'

Jack wished he could turn back down the path but he'd already run away once today. Where

Ruby was concerned he had no control over his mouth, his mushy brain or in fact any part of his body. He should never have returned. Having left once this afternoon, he should've stayed gone— from her home, from her private life. For the next four months. Until he left for Antarctica in the summer.

'Want a coffee or a beer?'

A peace offering? 'Beer, thanks. The amount of caffeine you drink you must be wired.' Maybe that was why she had kissed him back so readily.

Believe that and he'd believe pigs really did fly. She'd enjoyed kissing him as much as he'd enjoyed kissing her. Returning here was akin to walking through a pack of hungry lions. The sooner they'd done the job, the better for his sanity. Then he'd go home, turn on the computer and start seriously looking into jobs overseas for next year.

CHAPTER FIVE

THROUGH his office window Jack watched Ruby sliding out of her truck in the parking lot on Wednesday morning. Those short legs looked good in her jumpsuit, her heavy boots cute on her tiny feet. There was a line across her mouth-watering backside, probably made by her tucked-in undershirt. The stubborn set of her shoulders caused his mouth to curve upwards. Woe betide anyone who argued with Ruby today. What had brought that attitude on? Her shocking hair stood upright, no doubt glued into place with a hand-ful of hair gel.

Outrageously gorgeous. That was Red. Ruby. The pen he held spun across the room. Get a grip. They were about to spend the day working to-gether. *Her name is Ruby.*

Despite two days thinking about little else, he was still flummoxed as to why he'd kissed her. Other than being sidetracked by all that gorgeousness, that sexiness, her warmth and compassion. When she'd wrapped her arms around him in a sincere attempt to cheer him up he'd been doomed. He'd known he'd missed her, but that hug had brought need slamming through him. Need for Ruby. Need that would not take a back seat to his professional demands, or to his decision to remain buddies with her. Need that he might've thought had eased off since he'd last seen her but was now screaming around his veins with very little restraint.

On Monday he'd helped her finish the floor and then hightailed it for the pub and a few well-earned beers with Johnny, who had been home for ten days. It hadn't done any good at all. Not even spending most of yesterday at the aero club had doused his ardour for Ruby one iota.

But what had really frightened him was the thing slowly unfurling in his gut. Something that wasn't physical, more a sense of belonging to—with—Red. Like a light at the end of a long, dark corridor. Frighteningly like she was his beacon. As though he needed her for stability in his life. That revelation had come in the early hours of the morning, terrifying him.

He was the strong one around here, the man people came to for support, love and care. His fingers dug into his palms. He didn't need his own personal rock to lean on. Especially one in the form of a tiny, feisty redhead. But slowly it was dawning on him that Ruby was the counterbalance to all the haywire parts of him. She might be able to save him from his crazy schemes, such as chucking in his dream job to go off on a tangent. Or attempting to become a man he didn't recognise. He sure didn't recognise himself as someone about to start wandering the globe.

A slow sigh leaked over his bottom lip. Last night he'd driven past her house, drawn by an invisible thread. When he'd found the place in darkness a rare spurt of loneliness had gripped him, hollowed him out. Then he'd spent the rest of the night wondering where she was. Who she was with.

Ruby disappeared from sight around the corner of the building, and Jack took the moment to collect himself. This had to work, for both of them. Which meant no more hot kisses. Kisses were what had started this whole weird thinking about rocks and beacons, and kept him awake all night.

He heard Chris ask her, 'How was the rest of your time off?'

Ruby chuckled. 'Smashing, thanks.' She was coming closer to the office and Jack braced himself.

Chris asked, 'Oh, great. What did you take your hammer to?'

'That old wood shed. It was already falling down and only taking up space I want for planting spuds in spring.'

Planting spuds in spring? In time for Christmas dinner? When he'd be at Scott Base, freezing. Jack's spare pen snapped in his hand.

Chris continued, 'Did you get all that vinyl up?'

'Every last square inch of the blasted stuff, with Jack's help.' And there she was, standing in his doorway, studying him with a definite caution in those jade eyes. 'Morning, Jack.'

'Hi, there. So what's next to do in the kitchen?'

'The floor's being sanded tomorrow, earlier than I expected, so here's hoping for a fine weekend when I can start bringing those kauri boards to life.' Her eyes sparkled, caution forgotten as she bounced on her toes. 'It's going to look so cool.'

Jack asked, 'When does the builder put in your new cupboards?' Keep the conversation focused on everyday matters and he might make it through the first hour.

'Not sure about that. A week or two, I think. Longer than originally planned, anyway, since we took out that false ceiling.' Ruby shrugged. 'Are you coming with me to do a stocktake of our drugs? We do our bags before team two as the storeroom's too small for all of us at once.'

Anywhere would be too small with Ruby there, but he couldn't avoid the job. It was imperative to complete it efficiently and quickly. Jack pushed back his chair. 'Of course. Dave mentioned that's a priority for our first day on.'

'Dave's here, then?' Ruby asked over her shoulder as she headed for the locked storeroom where their packs were kept when not in use.

'He's over talking to Sandra about a malfunctioning light in number two 'copter.' Jack's gaze encompassed the compact woman he was following. The shapeless jumpsuit shouldn't make her look so delectable, but the way she cinched the waist in with a wide, non-uniform belt caused the fabric to flare softly over her tiny hips. And made his mouth go dry.

Ruby punched in the access code and tugged the door wide. She must've used up all the air in the small room because from the moment he entered Jack couldn't breathe. And when Red hauled their packs out backwards from a low cupboard she bumped up against his legs, causing Jack's heart to thump hard against his ribs. And he was supposed to work with her?

'Sorry,' she muttered, her cheeks flaming.

'Not a problem.' Sure thing, buddy. No problem at all. He reached around her for a pack and swung it up onto the small table.

Glaring at him, no doubt for intervening, she waited, hands on hips, while he unzipped one and spread the two sides out wide.

'Check the expiry dates first, right?' he asked, ignoring her rising irritation and carefully keeping far enough away so as not to inadvertently touch her.

Ruby picked up the stock list and pulled a pen from her pocket. 'You got it. Call them out and

I'll sign them off.' She leaned against the furthest wall. Still not far enough away.

The routine quickly settled Jack's oddly whacking heart and solved his breathing problems, but he knew it wouldn't last. Ruby had always rattled him. The only mistake he'd made had been to think he would no longer be affected by her. Oh, and taking a job where he had to work alongside her. Add in kissing her the other day and he had quite a list, considering this was his first official day on duty.

Ruby slipped the stock list back onto its hook, surprised her fingers were steady. Nothing else about her was. Her stomach was doing miniskips. Her heart rate pattered way too fast. And her tongue kept doing circuits of her mouth.

And whose fault was this? Jack Forbes. That was who. He should've withdrawn from the job when he'd learned she held a position at Rescue Helicopters. How was she supposed to work with him when she couldn't think straight whenever he was within touching distance? When they weren't squeezed into this cupboard of a storeroom they'd be crammed together in the back of the helicopter. Or sitting opposite each other in the tearoom.

'Anything else we need to do right now?' Jack's husky voice broke through her turmoil. The texture of his words had always excited her, especially when it came as a whisper near her ear.

'No.' She blinked. Slid towards the door and bumped slap bang into the man she was trying to avoid.

His hands gripped her shoulders. 'Steady.'

That husky voice sent shivers down her spine. Flipping her head back, she locked eyes with Jack. His mouth so close she only had to rise up on her toes, slide her hands around his neck to tug him closer and they'd be kissing again. He looked good enough to eat. Male, virile, exciting. Her breasts ached sweetly as she imagined his hands caressing them.

'Red?' Her nickname slid slowly off his tongue.

'Nothing.' Ruby jerked back and all but ran from the storeroom, not looking at Jack. Light drizzle had begun falling and as she made her way to the 'copter she shivered. A sharp southerly was rapidly approaching, bringing icy air. The one thing she didn't enjoy about being back home was winter. Wellington was living up to its cold and windy reputation. For a brief moment she missed San Francisco, even the fog-enshrouded days, then dismissed the sensation. Wellington was home, which meant dealing with the good and bad. Which meant dealing with facing the truth about her feelings for Jack. She might be falling in love with him all over again, but it didn't necessarily follow that he wanted her. Apart from in bed, because that had been so obvious back there, crammed together in the storeroom. His eyes had practically told her. But that was sex, not love. If Jack couldn't find it in his heart to love her again then it was just as well he was going away soon.

And then what? Slumping onto the jump seat, she tasted fear in her mouth. Had she made a mistake, coming back here? She'd so wanted to make a home for herself in this city where she had some wonderful memories of her time with Jack. Even of her mother and grandfather. She couldn't run now. She had to stop somewhere and she'd chosen Wellington. Had to stay long enough to see her vegetables grow, to finish her house and live in it. But what if Christmas arrived and loneliness drove her away in search of people to fill her days with? She'd always been hoping Jack would be around then. What if she really couldn't stay in one place, especially without Jack to anchor her?

Be strong, be tough. Her slump straightened a little. She could do this. She had to for her own sake. If she couldn't look out for herself, how could she expect anyone else to help her, love her, share her life with her? Her shoulders dragged back. Be strong, be tough. She had Zane. He'd be ecstatic to share the Christmas ham bone with her.

The clicks of switches up front as Chris and Slats ran through their daily checks reminded Ruby she did have friends here. She'd like to talk to Chris, ask him how long he'd lived here and did he think he'd stay working for the helicopter rescue unit, but she knew better than to talk to him now. The only time she ever saw him get cross was when someone bowled up and started yakking in his ear while he ran through his lists. He'd once told her that checks were a very important part of flying and he preferred total concentration otherwise he'd spend the day worrying he'd missed out something vital to a flight. So no interruptions. Anyway, what could he tell her that would put her at ease? He'd got his life together, had his dream job, a wonderful partner.

Yeah, and, Ruby, you've got your dream job, your house and a wonderful, wacky dog. Don't be greedy. Don't tempt fate to bring it all crashing down on your head because you're afraid to relax and make the most of those things. Get to work and stop daydreaming.

Vigorously scrubbing the stretcher with anti-bacterial cleaner, Ruby became immersed in the routine of her day, and Jack was finally on the back burner in her mind.

'Quiet day so far.' Chris poked his head around the bulkhead half an hour later, startling her. 'Jack seems an okay guy. You getting on with him?'

Sitting back on her haunches, Ruby considered the real question behind Chris's query. He probably wasn't the only one wondering if her previous relationship with Jack might sour things for everyone else. 'It's a bit early to comment on that. We've only had one afternoon together on the 'copter.' And one hot kiss. 'But having worked with him in A and E, I know he's a dedicated and skilled doctor. He's exacting, and doesn't suffer fools or shoddy work.'

Slats called from beside Chris, 'You'll be okay, then. Everyone says you're a very good paramedic.'

A compliment from Slats was rare. Heat spilled across her cheeks. 'Why, thank you, sir. As long as Jack thinks so.'

'Is that a general wish? Or a personal one?' Chris asked.

Ruby flipped her head up. 'What do you mean by that?' Had he guessed her feelings for their new boss? Not possible when she wasn't overly sure herself. Crikey, did everyone on the station think something was going on between her and Jack? Her hands fisted. Worse, had Jack heard anyone talking about them? That would definitely put him in a tailspin.

'Relax, Red.'

She bared her teeth at the use of that nickname. 'Don't.'

Chris chuckled. 'I rest my case. When Jack uses Red you don't bat an eyelid.' As a scowl began squeezing up her face he winked. 'It's okay, Ruby, your secret's safe. And for the record, I think it's time you had some fun.'

'I'm having heaps of fun. Look at what I'm doing with my house. That's the most amazing and exciting thing I've ever done. And I've got Zane, remember?' And the nights were long and lonely.

'I can't see you letting a dog snuggle up on your bed on a cold night.'

How true. She loved her mutt to bits but there were rules and sleeping in the laundry on his blankets was one. 'Yeah, well, I'm hardly going to let Jack snuggle up with me either.'

'For now.' Chris grinned, and ducked to avoid the plastic airway tube Ruby threw at him. He caught it effortlessly and tossed it back. 'You give yourself away every time.'

'True.' According to other people, she was an easy read. Jack had certainly always known what was on her mind, sometimes before she did. But he hadn't always got it right. He hadn't seen how desperately she'd wanted him to ask her to wait for him to go with her to the States. Unable to put her need into words, she'd relied on him working it out himself. Of course he hadn't. Could he still see through her? This Jack seemed more unsettled than the man she'd once loved. He'd always been very focused on reaching the top in his career as quickly as possible. She'd never doubted he'd make head of department. So why had he quit? What had happened that had pushed him away from that dream and into rescue work? Leaping out of an aircraft didn't seem to match the picture she held of a grounded, dedicated doctor like Jack.

A doctor who nowadays joined in with the crew for tea breaks and after-work socialising. He'd not done that when they'd worked in A and E, preferring to keep work and his private life separate. And he certainly wouldn't have turned up at the home of any staff member to help pull out cupboards.

She'd questioned him once. *'How can you justify having an affair with me when I'm a trainee nurse on your team?'*

'Why wouldn't I? You're my girlfriend. I love you.' That was all there was to it in his eyes. He'd continued to keep that side of their relationship separate from their working one, while

she'd often crossed his boundaries and earned his wrath.

The helicopter rocked as a sharp gust of wind buffeted it. Ruby glanced outside. 'Great. The drizzle is now horizontal rain. Should make for interesting flying conditions.'

Chris said, 'That front's coming in a lot faster than forecast. Hopefully it'll pass through as quickly. But the wind's predicted to get worse first.'

'Just as well we're quiet, then.' Ruby straightened up. 'Guess I'm going to get soaked going back inside. Want a coffee?'

'Might as well. Nothing happening out here.' Chris squeezed his broad shoulders through the narrow gap into the body of his 'copter and slid the door open.

Up front the radio crackled. Slats read out, 'Rescue Helicopter Crew Two, pick up MVA, Hutt highway, southbound, one POB, stat three.'

Ruby muttered, 'At least some of us have got something to do.' Crew Two usually took the less serious cases, leaving her crew on standby for the stat four or five calls.

'Be grateful. They're not going to have a comfortable flight.' Chris dropped to the ground and dashed to the building.

Ruby raced after him, cursing the numerous puddles. 'Have a rough trip, guys.' She waved as she passed Jason, Kevin and Cody heading out to their 'copter.

'It'll be a picnic,' Cody quipped.

Jack held the door open. Had he been watching out for them? 'Hot savouries and cake in the tearoom. My shout since it's my first proper day on the job.'

'Glad you've studied the rules for new staff.' Ruby shook herself like a wet spaniel, water droplets from her hair flying all around. 'I hate this weather.'

'Toughen up, Red. What's a bit of water?' Jack's smile was full of caution.

'Shut that door, will you?' she retorted. Straightening her shoulders, she turned for the tearoom, shivering as the cold air from the still open outside door swirled around her. 'Winter's the pits.'

And so was denying her attraction for her boss.

The day dragged. No major emergencies. Not even a minor one for Crew One to attend while Crew Two was busy. Ruby attacked the storeroom, scrubbing the already sparkling shelves, straightening the already straight lines of equipment.

The book she'd begun reading during her days off lay in her locker. Normally she'd have finished her chores and then sat in the staffroom reading that or studying current medical procedures, but today she was avoiding Jack who, with Dave, was working in there. They'd spread files and papers over the table, taking up all the available space. Eager to avoid Jack as much as possible, Ruby struggled to fill in her time elsewhere. When she could not avoid the staffroom any longer, she cranked up the spare computer to go online and order some books.

'What are you smiling about?' Jack asked from across the room.

She started, looked around. Where had Dave gone? 'Nothing.' He'd never believe her if she told him what she'd ordered.

Jack watched her closing down the website. 'Did you finally catch up with your father in the States?' he asked suddenly.

'Yep.' Double click on her email site.

'Not as good as you'd hoped?'

'Nope.' Five new emails.

Jack continued watching her. 'I'd like to know, Ruby. He was like a hovering black cloud that had to pass before our relationship could grow.'

'That's true.' The vet had sent a notice reminding her Zane was due for a check-up. She raised her head, peered at Jack. 'All right,' she muttered. 'The man I tracked down is my biological father, nothing more. He's a two-timing sleazeball that I'm ashamed to have wasted so many years daydreaming about. Mum was well shot of him.'

Click. Reply to the vet. *Please make me an appointment for next Monday.* Click. 'And so am I.'

A warm hand curled around her shoulder. Strong fingers squeezed gently. 'I'm sorry, Red, really sorry. I know how much you needed him to be a great dad.'

Click. Close the program. Log off. 'We don't always get what we want.'

Pushing her chair back, Ruby stood up, forcing Jack to remove his hand. She didn't need sympathy. Especially not from the man she'd hurt in order to find the Greaser.

'Red, remember that black night I came home

after A and E had been swamped in casualties from a train and bus accident?'

Ruby's eyes latched on to Jack's. Horror rolled through her as a dreadful scene bowled into her head. Jack crying. Jack shocked. Jack believing he could've saved more lives than he already had. Jack swearing he'd give up medicine the very next day.

'Red?' A feather-light touch on her chin. 'You listened to me for hours that night. You wrapped your arms around me and rocked me like a baby. You refused to let me feel sorry for myself.' Jack's eyes were enormous, and filled with...love?

No, not that. Understanding. That's it. Understanding. 'I remember,' she whispered.

'You saved me that night.'

'Yeah, I guess I did.'

'No one else has ever done something like that for me. Ever.' His finger slid up her chin, over her mouth. 'I'll always be around for you.'

Except you're going away. Gulp. Pain burned in her throat, her stomach. Did he know how much she longed to throw herself at him and tell him of her shame over hurting him for the sake of the Greaser?

Well, she wasn't going to. She couldn't. He might feel sorry for her. Straightening up, she stepped away, refusing to be drawn in by his sympathetic gaze. She couldn't afford to go there. Jack might be offering to help her in the bad times but he wasn't staying around for *all* the times. The good, bad and indifferent times.

'Thanks, Jack. Glad to know I've got good mates.' She'd go and annoy Julie until the shame burning her gut dissipated.

Jack watched her go, hurting for her, hurting for them. They'd had a good thing going in the past. They'd connected in a way, not as close and honest as it should've been but there'd been the basis for it getting better.

What had happened between her and her father? If only she'd talk to him about it.

Huh? Ruby should talk to you? As in the guy who never told her anything more important than where to meet him after work?

Jack shivered. Any right he had to help Red was long gone. He'd made a right pig's breakfast of things back then. And still was.

That was because he didn't know what he was

doing with his life any more. This grand plan to get out and see the world was already stuttering to a halt. Working on the helicopters still excited him. He was looking forward to that. And going to Scott Base.

It's the other stuff he couldn't get his head around. Life outside work. Ruby stuff. How could he sort out her problems when he couldn't deal with his own? She didn't need a basket case in her life.

His cellphone vibrated in his pocket. Flipping it open, he saw the caller was his mate from the paediatric ward at Wellington Hospital. 'Hey, Ian, what've you got for me?'

A few minutes later he found Ruby sitting on the floor of Julie's office, screeds of patient reports lying over and around her legs. 'Hey, what are you doing down there?'

'Making myself useful.' She didn't look up.

'I see.' She was trying to avoid him. Fair enough. He couldn't find fault with that. 'I thought you'd like to know that Lily Byrne regained consciousness this morning.'

Ruby raised her head sharply. 'That's fantastic

news. Do the doctors know if she's going to be a hundred per cent all right?'

'Too soon to know. They've got a whole battery of tests lined up to do over the next few days. But at least Lily's situation is improving.'

The reports spilled from Ruby's fingers as she stopped sorting them into alphabetic order. 'Her parents must be feeling more hopeful. How is Lily's mother, do you know?'

'She's well enough to have been transferred from Hutt Hospital into Wellington. She's thrilled to be closer to Lily but until the results of all those tests are known there'll be no relaxing for those parents.' Sadness gripped him as memories of Beth's accident assailed him. Every time he dealt with an accident involving a child he went through this pain of wanting to make everything work out all right for the families involved. Every time it didn't he felt the agony the families were going through.

On his belt his pager vibrated. At last. A job. 'We're on, Ruby. Let's hustle.'

CHAPTER SIX

'DESTINATION Rapara Island.' Ruby looked up as wind rattled the window. 'Ripper stuff. We're about to get slam-dunked all over the sky as we cross Cook Strait.' The island was part of the Marlborough Sounds at the top of the South Island. A beautiful spot in summer, isolated and harsh in winter. 'Let's move.'

Jack read from his pager, '"Forty-one-year-old female. Premature labour at thirty-one weeks, heavy bleeding."'

'Buckle up tight,' Chris told them as they scrambled inside the helicopter.

'What's the forecast for the next two hours?' Jack asked him.

'Wind should be abating by now, so here's hoping it sees fit to do just that. I'm guessing this won't be a quick transfer?'

'Can't answer that until I've examined the woman,' Jack answered, 'but I'll—' He stopped, nodded at Ruby. 'Sorry, we'll be as quick as safely possible.'

Ruby tugged her safety harness tight and leaned her head back, closing her eyes.

'You okay?' Jack asked as his harness buckle clicked into place.

'Yes.' She added in a softer tone, 'Just running through what I know about prem babies and what we can expect.'

'I wish we had a few more details, such as is the mother having regular contractions? Who decided she was even in labour? Is she panicking because of the bleeding?' When Ruby opened her eyes and stared at him, Jack was quick to snap, 'That's not a criticism, merely a concern. I'm guessing living out on Rapara Island would automatically crank up the worry scale for any pregnant woman, and especially one in her forties.'

'The woman probably intended being off the island well before her due date. I wonder if she has other children or if it's a first pregnancy.'

'Let's hope not. She'll at least understand what's happening if she's been through it before.' Jack rested his elbows on his knees, his chin on his tightly interlaced fingers. 'Okay, what steps do we take when we arrive?'

Ruby ran down the list. 'First the usual obs—BP, resp rate, temperature in case of infection, listen for the foetal heartbeat.' She tapped her fist on her thigh. 'Oh, and time any contractions.'

The helicopter lurched and Ruby gripped the sides of her jump seat, calling out to Chris, 'Hey, if I wanted a roller-coaster ride I'd have gone to the theme park.'

'Just saving you the air fare to Auckland,' Chris quipped, before adding, 'So much for the wind dropping. I can see the *Kaitaki* down below. Those passengers will be having the trip from hell.'

'I'd have refused to go,' Ruby called back. 'I'm not keen on the ferry on a flat, calm day.'

Jack's brow creased. 'You get seasick?'

'Prostrate with nausea.'

'You did okay when we lifted that cardiac arrest patient off the other day.'

'Had other things on my mind.' Like saving a patient's life.

'Rapara coming up,' Chris called. 'There's a vehicle with flashing lights below the ridge.

Hopefully that means we'll be sheltered as we go in.'

Within minutes Ruby and Jack were squashed into the cab of a four-wheel-drive vehicle with their patient's husband and bouncing across paddocks to the farmhouse. Every bump caused their thighs to rub against each other. Every sway of the truck banged their arms together. Ruby clenched her jaw, hoping they'd reach their destination soon. She heard Jack's sharp intake of breath. So she wasn't the only one suffering.

'Mary got backache late yesterday,' Colin Archer said in response to Jack's brusque questioning. 'She wanted to get off the island and go to Blenheim where our GP is but then her back came right. I had to go over to the other side to muster sheep and she said she'd be fine. Should've known better and taken her out then. It's my fault she's in the state she is.'

Jack sighed. 'We'll soon have Mary on the way to hospital. Don't go blaming yourself for anything, just concentrate on being calm and cheerful for your wife.'

'Just like that, eh?' The other man rolled his eyes at Jack, before leaning over the steering-wheel to peer through the murk. 'There's the house. Mary's probably still pacing the floor. I tried to make her lie down but she got mad at me, said I didn't know a thing about having a baby and to get out of the house. Guess this is a bit more complicated than lambing my ewes.'

Ruby bit down on a sudden smile. 'Is this your first baby, then?'

'We're latecomers. Got married less than a year ago and tried for a family straight away. Took a few goes till we got it right.' Colin winked, then his mouth dropped again. 'I should never have brought Mary out here until after the little blighter was born. But she insisted, even learned to drive the boat in case she had to take herself to town to see the GP.'

Jack asked, 'So when did your wife last see her doctor?'

'Some time in March, I think it was.'

And this was June. Ruby shook her head slightly. The woman should've been seeing her GP regularly. 'Has Mary had other children?'

'No, none at all. She was too busy working on her career as an international journalist to be having kids. Found it hard to stop here at first but she's learned to ride the tractors, dock the sheep. Turning into a right little farmer she is.'

If an international journalist could make a life for herself out here where there was absolutely nothing but animals then surely she could handle Wellington, Ruby mused. And maybe she could find a way back to Jack.

Mary Archer met them at the back door, her hands tucked under her very pregnant belly. Her face was grey, her eyes dull. 'Sorry for all the bother but I think I'm in trouble,' she said after they'd introduced themselves.

Jack didn't waste any time. 'Can we go through to your bedroom so I can examine you? Tell me why you think you're in labour.'

'I'm getting regular pains, Doc. Here.' She stabbed her abdomen. 'My back's been giving me grief since last night. There's been lots of blood. My baby will be all right, won't it?' Her teeth dug into her lower lip.

'Let's take things one step at a time. How far apart are your pains?' Jack helped the woman onto the unmade bed.

'About five minutes, I reckon. I haven't been

timing them. Figured there was no point. If it's coming, it's coming.'

Ruby unzipped the pack and pulled out the blood-pressure cuff. Around the other side of the bed she reached for Mary's arm. 'Has your blood pressure been normal throughout your pregnancy?'

'In March the doc said it was fine for a pregnant lady.'

Which told them absolutely nothing. Mary wouldn't have been to antenatal classes either. She could be in for a shock. Did she know how to breathe her way through the contractions? Ruby wrote the BP reading on her glove, too low, and showed it to Jack. 'I'm going to take your temperature, Mary. Then I'll check your glucose level.' Pregnancy diabetes could be a further complication.

Jack made an internal examination. Then he listened for a foetal heartbeat. As Ruby watched him his brow creased. What? No heartbeat? Oh, hell.

'Two beats.' Jack grinned at Ruby. 'Two.' He looked to his patient. 'Mary, have you had a scan since becoming pregnant?'

'No. I've avoided all those things. I guess you're going to tell me off.'

Jack shook his head. 'It's too late for that. But we need to get you to hospital ASAP. I think you're having twins. Which would partially explain the early labour.'

'Twins?' Mary gaped at Jack.

'Twins?' bellowed her husband from the doorway, causing Ruby to jump with shock. She'd forgotten all about the poor man. 'You mean we're having two babies? But we're not geared for two. We've only got one crib, and one set of clothes, and…' His voice dwindled from a roar to a whisper. 'Hell, who'd have thought, eh?'

'You'll have plenty of time to go shopping,' Ruby told him. 'If these two arrive today, they'll be in hospital for a little while.'

Mary groaned as another contraction gripped her.

Ruby wiped Mary's forehead and held her hand. She was sure that all her metatarsals would be broken in the bigger woman's ferocious grasp. 'You're doing well,' she tried to reassure the mother-to-be.

'Try not to push,' Jack told Mary. 'I'm going to

give you a drug that will hopefully delay delivery at least until we get you to hospital. I'll top it up every thirty minutes.'

Ruby retrieved a vial from the pack and handed it to Jack.

Mary gasped, 'Are you taking me to Nelson Hospital?'

'Sorry, it's Wellington for you,' Ruby told her.

'But my GP's in Nelson. My family are there. My friends.'

Ruby helped her sit up and swing her legs over the side of the bed. 'I'm sure you'll be transferred to Nelson later on, but first we need to get you to proper care and Wellington is closer.' The difference in distance wasn't too much but Ruby hoped to calm Mary because there was no choice in their destination. 'You do want what's best for those little ones, don't you?'

'Of course. I just never thought I'd be going anywhere else.' Her eyes widened. 'How will Colin get there? Is there room in the helicopter for him?'

'Unfortunately not,' Ruby replied. 'We need the space in case you start to deliver.'

Mary stood up awkwardly, her thighs pressed

together, as though afraid her babies might drop out. 'But I need Colin with me.'

'I'll leave in the boat the moment you're airborne, love,' Colin tried to reassure her.

'What happens if the babies decide to come while we're flying?' Mary asked.

Ruby had never seen such a white face.

Jack's brow puckered, his eyes narrowed. The look he got while trying to think of how to word something so as not to upset anyone. It was such a familiar expression that Ruby's heart tipped sideways. The last time she'd seen that look had been when he'd told her, 'Goodbye, hope it all works out for you.'

'I've delivered a few babies in my time. We'll manage, okay? Try to relax.' He smiled that smile that usually won over even the most stubborn people. 'You're thinking what would I know about what you're going through? Right?'

Outside Ruby clambered onto the back of the truck, leaving Jack to squeeze in beside his patient. 'You okay back there?' he asked. 'I can swap places.'

'You're needed inside. I'll be fine. It's only a short ride.' Ruby sat down on a very wet pile of sacks just as Colin lurched the vehicle forward. She grabbed for a rail and held on. Cold moisture seeped into her jumpsuit, making her shiver. *Great. Now I'll look like I've wet myself.*

On board the helicopter they quickly made Mary comfortable. Then, as Chris and Slats began the start-up procedure, Ruby called Wellington Hospital A and E on the radio and filed Mary's details so the appropriate staff and equipment would be waiting for them when they touched down.

The next thirty-five minutes took for ever as they banged into a strong headwind. Every time Mary groaned, Ruby held her breath. A mid-air birth would not be fun for any of them. Slowly the drug took effect and the contractions abated. But for how long?

She took another BP reading and showed it to Jack. 'No change.'

He nodded. 'You're doing fine, Mary.' Sitting back on his haunches he mused, 'Twins, eh? Double trouble. Or double fun. I reckon it would be great to have two babies at once.'

Ruby gaped at him. 'You'd like twins?' When had he decided he'd like babies at all? They had never discussed having children. Her heart sank. What had they learned about each other? Absolutely nothing, it seemed.

'If I was having children, yes, I reckon I would. They'd always have a mate, someone who understood them, someone to look out for them all the time.'

'Like you and Steve?'

'Something like that but more.' A far-away look washed through his eyes, lightening their slate-grey colour. Had Jack missed out on friends while he was growing up? Had his life been dedicated to making sure his father and brother were happy? So that they didn't leave him?

She couldn't ask him. He'd turn away from her, his eyes would snap with disapproval. So Ruby nudged him. 'And what about the extra work? All those nappies, all the extra bottles of milk, the crying late at night when one wakes the other?'

'I'd be there, doing my share.' He turned that dreamy gaze on her. 'Don't you ever think about having a family of your own, Red?'

Stunned, Ruby could only swallow and shake her head. He'd said babies and Red in the same sentence. Did that mean anything? Or nothing?

She sank back on her seat and reached for the safety harness. No, she was getting way ahead of the ball. 'Can't say I have.' She had enough on her plate with the house and Zane.

Sure she did. Her eyes scoped Jack. An unbidden thought unfolded, expanded, took hold. Kids. Her very own children. With Jack. Wow. This was something she'd never considered, didn't know what to do with.

Because it was never, ever, going to happen. Children, with or without Jack. How did a woman who'd given her mother such a hard time bring up her own children?

A few hours ago she'd ordered cookery books that she didn't know how to use. How could she raise kids? For starters, they'd need feeding. How old did they have to be before they ate pizza?

No, no, no. Maybe she needed to go back to the SPCA and get Zane a playmate. Two dogs should keep her few free hours full, and at least she could buy them ready-made dog food.

Just over a week later, Julie placed a courier package on the tearoom table in front of Ruby after they'd handed over to the next shift. 'This arrived for you today. You and your books. You're going to have to build a library in your house.'

Ruby smiled happily. All taken care of. Three shelves in one of her new kitchen cupboards would be allocated to recipe books. She lifted the parcel, felt the weight of the books. Solid hard-cover ones. 'The bathroom's next. I'm not living through another winter without fixing that up. I get into a piping-hot shower at five in the morn-ing, then snap-freeze the moment I step back out.' She shivered exaggeratedly. 'How did peo-ple survive eighty years ago?'

'They were hardy.' Jack tugged open the fridge and handed around beers, putting one back when Ruby shook her head. He sat on the opposite side of the room and looked around at all his colleagues, except Ruby. 'What's everyone got planned for their days off?'

'I'm going to sit in my new kitchen and gloat.' Ruby tipped her chair onto its back legs. He mightn't be looking at her but she could still an-swer. 'If it's finished.'

'How many days has that taken?' Jack asked.

'Three.' Every night she'd gone home and stood in the middle of her changing kitchen space and absorbed the clean blue and white lines of her new cabinets. And last night she'd rubbed her hands over the sensuously smooth, black granite benchtops.

'We should have a kitchen-warming party,' Chris supplied.

'What? And have you lot tramping around on my beautifully varnished floor?'

'Are you actually going to use this kitchen?' Jack asked. 'As in turn the stove on, cook meals?'

Just you wait and see, she gloated to herself. Which reminded her. What was the time? Oops, time to go. She leapt up. 'Must fly. Things to do, places to be.'

'You're not coming to the pub for a meal?' Jack looked around the room. 'Isn't that what we're all doing?'

'Rain-check.' Ruby nipped over to her locker and tugged out her bag as everyone else confirmed they were on for the pub. 'See you all next week. Enjoy the days off.'

Out in the car park she swung up into her truck. She had to go to the supermarket, walk Zane and change out of her uniform, all in less than an hour.

Jack's face appeared at her side window and she lowered it reluctantly. Any delay would have a serious impact on her plans. 'Yes?'

'What's the hurry?'

She wanted to keep the cookery lessons secret until she'd mastered a few simple techniques. 'I'm running late. I'll get growled at if I don't get a wriggle along.'

'Oh, sorry, didn't mean to keep you.' Jack stepped back, looking as though she'd slapped him.

'You're not.' Ruby smiled, trying to erase that frown between his eyebrows. Putting the gearshift into drive, she added, 'Have a good two days off. See you later.'

Her wheels spun on the wet tarmac as she sped away. She winced, screwing up her face. Now Jack would really think her date was extra-hot. She glanced at him in the rear-view mirror. Oh, hell. He stood staring after her, an angry figure in the partially dark car park, her courier package in his hand. The books she'd forgotten in her rush to get away.

CHAPTER SEVEN

THE following morning, package in hand, Jack wandered through Ruby's front yard towards the back of the house, wondering why he was bothering. It was obvious from last night that Ruby had a life that had no place in it for him. Had she been on a hot date? He fervently hoped not.

But he'd seen that glint of excited anticipation in Ruby's eyes yesterday when Julie had handed over the parcel and knew she'd want it. Yeah, right. Any excuse to see her. Whether he'd be welcome was a very different story.

But today he felt oddly ready to take some chances. Nothing he could explain, but it was almost as though he had unfinished business with Ruby. When she'd headed to the States he'd believed their break-up was final with no chance of a reunion later on. Any time someone had left him it had been final. Like the day his sister had died. That had been a cold day in hell even for a seven-year-old. A cold day followed by a cold week and an even chillier year. He'd missed Beth so much. Her cheeky grin, the way she'd hung around her brothers all the time.

Then there'd been his mum. Distraught beyond belief with the loss of Beth, she'd gradually fallen apart right before his eyes. The laughter and fun that had been her trademark had never returned. Then there'd been the day he'd woken to silence. Trotting through the house, he'd found every room empty. Mum had gone. Out in the garden his father sat hunched over, a forlorn figure with nothing left inside him to console his frightened son.

Some time in the following days and weeks Jack had learned to make himself indispensable to his father and to Steve. No one else would ever leave him behind again.

Until Ruby.

Her departure had been agony. Even as an adult he'd struggled to deal with it. Oh, he'd told himself he understood, but beneath his bravado he'd hurt badly. No matter how he'd cushioned the truth, Ruby had left him. And he hadn't put up a fight, any more than he had for Beth or his mum.

But now Ruby was back. Not for him. But she was here. And it was wonderful to see her. A living, vibrant Ruby. A calmer, happier Ruby. But his fledgling hopes of maybe spending time with her dived to his toes. She had history. History she was working hard to fix. But he'd seen the doubt float through her eyes when she'd hit problems with the kitchen. If Ruby didn't believe in herself, didn't trust that she'd make it, how was he supposed to?

Voices penetrated his dismal thoughts. Children? Surely not. Jack rounded the corner and Zane tore at him, barking crazily. Jack took the impact in his legs and leaned down to scratch behind the dog's ears. 'Hey, boy, slow down.'

'Who are you?' a young voice demanded.

Jack lifted his head and found himself staring directly into the quizzical faces of three boys. They stood shoulder to shoulder, assessing him. Were these guys the hot date? He chuckled. His shoulders lifted and he studied the trio. Did they think they were guarding Ruby? They all had blond, curly hair and the same piercing blue eyes, as well as similar miniature tough-man stances. 'I'm Jack. Who are you?'

'Are you Ruby's friend?' the tallest asked.

'Yes. We work together.' Jack straightened up.

'Are you a pilot?' the same boy asked, a flicker of excitement in his direct gaze.

How easy it would be to win this lot over. Jack shook his head. 'Sorry, I'm only a doctor.'

'Ruby's a sort of doctor,' he was told.

Another brother said, 'No, she's not. She's a para-thingy.'

'Paramedic,' Jack supplied. 'How old are you boys?'

'Seven.'

'Six.'

'Five.'

'What are your names?' They were kind of cute.

'Toby.'

'Thomas.'

'Tory.'

'Nice to meet you all. Where's Ruby?'

Toby stepped forward. Or was it Thomas? 'She's inside, making us hot chocolate.'

Jack hoped these kids had cast-iron stomachs. 'Sounds yummy.'

'Ruby makes the best chocolate drink. She puts marshmallows in it so they melt and go gooey.'

So the boys had survived previous drinks here. 'Think she'll have enough for me too?'

'Hey, Jack,' Ruby called out the kitchen window. 'You run out of things to do at your place?'

Nope. The lawn needed mowing. The recycling stuff required taking to the tip. The path could do with a sweep. And the basement would look better with a new coat of paint. 'Yeah, something like that.'

'He wants a hot chocolate,' one of the boys yelled, so loud Jack's ears reverberated.

'Lucky I've made a pot full, then. You'd all better come in. Take your gumboots off on the porch, boys. I don't want mud tramped inside my kitchen.'

'Ruby's fussy about the floor at the moment,' one boy told Jack with a serious face.

'You say the same things that Mum tells us,' Thomas grumbled at Ruby.

'Then I must be right.' Ruby grinned before shutting the window.

'You forgot your parcel in your hurry to get away last night.' Jack placed it on the table, trying not to stare at Ruby. Dressed in butt-hugging jeans and a green merino jersey that matched her eyes she appeared not much older than her young charges. The apprehension he'd felt since the day he'd learned he'd be working with Ruby unravelled a little.

'Thanks.' A faint pink hue coloured her cheeks.

As she took the package he quickly shoved his hands in his jacket pockets. No accidental touching today. 'Where do your little friends come from?'

'Over the road. I offered to have them while their parents go out for lunch and some couple time, which is pretty hard to get with these three little men.'

'That's a nice thing you're doing.'

Ruby handed him a mug of steaming chocolate with the anticipated marshmallows bobbing on top. 'It's not exactly taxing. The boys spend most of the time playing with Zane, which gives him extra exercise and wears him out for me.'

'It hasn't taken you long to establish yourself in the neighbourhood.' Envy stabbed him. He hadn't got to know any of his neighbours. Like him, they were all too busy building careers, and barely took the time to wave at each other when they put the trash cans out on Monday mornings.

'Knowing my neighbours is essential if I don't want to live in isolation. I want to be able to knock on the boys' door and invite them and their parents over for a barbecue in summer, or take Mrs Crocombe some new spuds for her dinner.'

'You've never had that, have you?' Jack recalled how Ruby used to watch families at the beach with such a hunger in her eyes he had always been surprised it hadn't devoured her. Even with his screwed-up family he'd felt he belonged in his community. Despite keeping aloof, he'd known deep down there were people who'd have helped him if he'd ever been desperate enough to ask.

Ruby handed drinks and a soft smile to each of the lads. 'I have now.'

One of the boys flicked a marshmallow into his mouth and grinned. 'Yummy, yummy, I've got mallow in my tummy.'

'Can we take Zane to the beach later?' Toby asked.

'Have you got warm jackets?' Ruby asked. At three solemn nods she said, 'Okay, sounds like a plan to me. Jack, want to join us?' Her breathing stopped as she waited for his reply.

'Count me in. We used to enjoy walking along the beach.' Holding hands, laughing.

'You always said you'd get a dog one day.'

'You beat me to it.' His gaze followed Ruby as she turned back to the bench, suddenly intent on wiping up some spilled water. Did work colleagues usually go to the beach with someone else's kids? Not exactly keeping his distance from Ruby. Another thought blinded him. When they'd first met and got together, had Ruby felt the sense of helplessness he did now? Had she fought getting involved? Had she even thought about how she'd eventually leave him? How well had they known themselves back then, let alone each other? He didn't know himself now. Six months ago, if someone had said he'd quit A and E, he'd have sent them for a brain scan.

Excited chatter filled the air. Jack tried to focus on the boys. They talked a foreign language, kid stuff, arguing and giggling as they slurped up liquid chocolate.

What he couldn't get his head around was how effortlessly Ruby handled them. They did everything she asked in preparation for leaving, finishing their drinks and putting the mugs in the sink without a single protest, gathering their jackets and getting into the back seat of the twin-cab truck.

Jack closed the back door of the truck and got in beside Ruby. The boys obviously adored her. Why wouldn't they? She was adorable. And funny, playful. What's more, she seemed to know exactly what they liked doing. If he had to pick a mother for his children, he'd choose Ruby.

Jack swore. Hard. Silently. His hand reached for the doorhandle. Going to leap out of the vehicle? He might land on his head and knock some sense into it. Something needed to. Was he crazy? Where did these weird ideas come from?

'Everyone belted up?' Impervious to his silent rant, Ruby glanced over at the boys and didn't engage the truck in gear until they'd all said yes, including him.

He watched as she carefully negotiated the busy Saturday-morning traffic, and said lamely, 'You love driving this truck, don't you?'

Tossing him a grin, she said, 'People actually take notice of me in this, especially as I'm darned fine at reversing. Men stand around watching, thinking I'm going to make a total clot of myself. I so love getting it right first go. Their jaws drop and they turn away in such a hurry they trip over themselves.'

Jack tried to laugh, but it stuck in his throat around the lump that had sprung up when it had struck him he wanted kids with this woman. 'You've never been invisible.'

Her eyes widened along with her grin. 'Thanks. I think.' She negotiated a speed bump in the road, glanced in the rear-view mirror. 'I don't like Zane being on the deck but he loves it.'

'He doesn't attempt to jump off?'

'He's chained up, but if I have to stop in a hurry he'll slam into the cab.' She slowed for a corner, turned onto Oriental Parade and parked by the beach. 'Here we go, guys. Everyone out. Watch for cars.'

'Bossy britches.' Jack slid out and opened the back door for the lads, who tumbled out in a flurry of arms and legs, shouting about who would take Zane's lead first.

Chuckling, Ruby took the lead herself. 'Last one on the beach is a smelly egg.'

Jack loped along behind everyone, making sure he was the egg and not little Tory, who had the shortest legs and was struggling to keep up with his brothers.

Sticks were thrown for Zane and naturally the boys tended to toss theirs towards the sea. Zane repaid them by shaking salt water over everyone. Finally Jack took the boys in hand. 'Let's skim stones over the water.'

'Yes, please,' three voices yelled.

'I'll take Zane to the end and back. Wear off some of his energy.' Ruby jogged away down the beach, leaving her charges in his hands.

He glanced after her in amazement. Ruby and exercise had never gone together before. She'd believed people only ran if they were being chased by something terrifying. So those firm muscles he'd felt the other day when he'd held her in his arms weren't just from swinging a hammer. No wonder she looked so delectable in her jumpsuit.

Jack spun away, heaved the stone in his hand across the wavelets as hard and far as he could. It slammed through the crest of the first wave and sank.

Thomas jumped up and down with glee. 'You got it wrong, you got it wrong.'

I sure did, buddy. I should've stayed at home and cut the lawns. Then I wouldn't have this melting sensation in my gut. Or feel power-less. I wouldn't be wondering how soon I can kiss Ruby again. Ruby, you're making my heart pound, making my knees knock, all over again. Tell me why I'm going away in October. Will you cry as I go through to the departure lounge, as I cried for you?

Jack looked as though he was thoroughly en-joying himself as he told the kids a joke about a hairy monster. Ruby shifted on the park bench, trying to get comfortable. It was spooky how right this felt. The kids and the dog and Jack. Cosy and warm. Like a family. She spluttered into her soda can. A repeat image of her and Jack and their babies slammed into her mind, brighter than before.

'Back off,' she growled under her breath. This was totally crazy. Jack needed a woman who could make him open up and share his feelings, something he'd never done with her. He needed a partner who'd be there all the time for him. Her fingers curled tight around the can. Her heart thumped a little harder. She'd had her chance, and she'd blown it. Jack didn't need her in his life. Whatever he chose to do in the future.

'What are you going to do after your stint at Scott Base?' she asked abruptly.

'I'm not sure yet. I've applied for a few jobs overseas.' He scrunched up a burger bag and tossed it at the rubbish bin. 'Nothing's really grabbed me yet, though.'

The soda can pinged as Ruby's fingers pressed a dent into it. How was it that when she finally stopped running and wanted to stay put, Jack had come up with this idea of going off to see the world? 'You never wanted to travel before.'

'Excuse me?' Jack's eyebrows shot upwards.

And when he continued to stare at her like she'd grown another head, she explained, 'I can't remember you ever mentioning going overseas. You always said you had too many commitments here for that. Your dad, Steve. Your career.'

'I did, didn't I?' The eyebrows slowly returned to normal. 'I can gain a lot of experience working in other countries.' He gathered up the boys' discarded wrappers and bags, stood up and tossed them into the bin.

So that was that. She could stop mooning about families and accept Jack had a very different agenda these days.

'Let's go.' Jack nodded at the boys and picked up Zane's lead.

'Sure,' she muttered as she followed them back to the truck. She hated it that he wouldn't talk to her about his plans, even as a friend. Wanting to know more about his life since she'd gone away, Ruby asked as she drove down the road, 'How's your dad? Still working for the immigration department?'

Jack settled himself into the corner, turning to face her. 'You'll never believe it but Dad's moved to Auckland.'

'Really?' Mr Forbes leaving Jack and Steve? Leaving the people who supported him? Wow.

'He met a lady when she came down here to work in the department and…' Jack snapped his fingers '…just like that he was head over heels in love. I wouldn't have believed it if I hadn't witnessed it. After twenty-three years on his own my father lost his heart.'

'Do you like this lady?' Mr Forbes had replaced one support system for another and in doing so had let Jack down.

'Absolutely. She's wonderful to Dad. The only snag was that he had to move to Auckland as she has commitments up there, but that didn't faze him at all.'

'You must miss him heaps.'

'I do but I can't begrudge him his happiness. You should see them together, like a couple of lovestruck teens.'

Ruby thought of the sombre man she'd known. 'I'm pleased for him. He deserved a break. So with your dad gone and Steve only here occasionally, you're free to do what you want now.'

No wonder Jack appeared restless. All the people he'd put first in his life had slipped off the radar. And he didn't know what to do with himself. A focused man when it came to his family and career who had no idea how to live his own life—for himself. Did he even know what he wanted?

'I always knew what I wanted.'

Reading her mind?

He continued, 'To be the best at emergency

medicine I could be. I've achieved that. Taking this temporary position might be a sideways step, but it's still emergency medicine.'

'You are happy, right?' She flicked a sideways glance at him and saw him blink.

'Why wouldn't I be?' He pushed against his seat.

'Something I'm sensing. Could be because I'm still getting used to the idea of you going away.'

'You're saying that what I set in motion as a teenager about to start med school has to remain my plan for ever?'

'Me? Hardly. Being the biggest changer of plans I've ever met, that would be hypocritical.' She sighed.

'You've certainly done a total rollover of your life. From upping sticks on a regular basis you now say you're putting down roots, never to disappear over the horizon again.'

Back to her and his disbelief that she might have changed. At least he had talked a little about his dad, a first in their relationship. 'Like I said, circumstances have altered. I should've listened to Mum.' A cold lump clunked in her stomach.

'It's probably natural that you never accepted her version of someone so important to you.'

'I was wrong.' The lump grew, rolled around her belly. 'This is where I was the closest to being content. Mum's buried here. I go talk to her every week. It would take something cataclysmic to move me out of Wellington now.' Mentally she crossed her fingers, afraid she'd tempted fate.

Jack's eyes bored into her as she turned into her street. What was his problem? She'd told him too much, but at least it was the truth. 'Ruby...' his voice caressed her '...I know how badly you wanted your father to be a part of your life.'

She stared at the road, blinking away the sudden mist in her eyes. That gentle understanding undid the lock on her determination to keep the sorry story to herself. 'It was worse than that.' Slowly a piece of her unravelled and she told him what she'd never told another soul. 'I did have a fairy-tale picture of my father. But it was a cover-up. Ever since I can remember I blamed myself for him leaving. I thought he hated me. I believed Mum's inability to make a home for us in one place was because she was heartbroken and looking for him.'

'He left before you were born. How could he hate you?'

Her mouth was bitter. 'He'd been calling on Mum whenever he came through Christchurch, until Mum got pregnant. She never saw him again once she told him. She went on the road, moving from town to town every couple of years. Once I was old enough to learn the facts, I blamed myself. Unfortunately those facts were totally skewed and fed to me by my grandfather, whom I adored.'

'He shouldn't have done that. You'd have been too vulnerable.'

'Granddad was bitter. His precious daughter heartbroken. He reacted as many loving fathers would.' But not hers. *He'd* never acknowledged her, not even when she'd tracked him down. Oh, no, he'd been terrified her appearance would wreck the comfortable life he'd built for himself using his trusting father-in-law's daughter and wealth. 'The Greaser deserves every last drop of Granddad's bitterness. And more.'

Jack's hand touched her leg, his fingers spread across her thigh in a gentle touch that warmed her and threatened to turn the mist to a flood of tears.

'You know something? You've come through this and you're different. Calmer, more sorted, if you know what I mean.' His hand remained on her leg. 'You've still got attitude, though.' And he muttered, 'Thank goodness.'

Did he like the new her? They used to get on so well, maybe he preferred the uptight, unhappy Ruby. Not likely. 'I feel as though a whole world of trouble has gone. My life's looking up and, yes, I'm content.'

Especially since Jack was in the truck with her, his warm hand so right as it touched her. Sharing the day with him had brought the sun out in her heart, despite getting carried away in the confession department. 'Thanks for spending the day with us,' she said, then added, 'You surprised me when you agreed to come.'

'Surprised myself.' Jack slowly removed his hand. 'It's been fun.'

In the back of the truck the boys were playing paper and scissors amid loud shrieks. Ruby grinned at them through the rear-view mirror. 'These guys are so cool, I love them.'

Jack glanced over his seat. 'You're right, they are. Bet they must be a handful for their parents at times. None of my friends have kids of an age that I can play with yet. They've all got babies, those that have got family.'

That reminded her. 'I wonder how Mary's twins are doing. They must've grown a teeny bit by now.'

'Shall we call into the hospital later? Do you ever do that with any of the patients you bring in?'

Ruby parked outside her gate, hauled on the handbrake, unclipped her belt. 'Sometimes. It depends on the situation, whether they were conscious and talking while I was with them. But I'd like to see those girls.' She laughed. 'Colin Archer won't know what's hit him when they all go home. In the space of a year he's gone from a lone man living on his island to having three females around the place.'

'Bet he has those girls delivering lambs before they're even talking.' Jack swung out of the truck and let the boys out before getting Zane down. Like he'd been doing this all his life.

Ruby watched him, her heart squeezing for the sad and troubled boy he must've been, the unsettled man he'd become. He'd had to watch out for Steve a lot while trying to make their father give them some space to grow up in. Apparently old man Forbes had lived in fear of losing his sons after his wife had gone away. According to Steve, he'd clung to the boys to the point he'd almost strangled them.

And now Jack's dad and Steve didn't need Jack like they used to. No wonder he was lost. Would he find whatever it was he wanted at the rescue base? Or at Scott Base? In another country?

Darn, she'd finally realised what she wanted more than anything. Not the job, the house or even, at a pinch, Zane, bless him. She wanted Jack, every little piece of him. And he was planning to disappear on her.

Ruby gazed in awe around the heaving pub Jack had brought her to on Courtney Place. 'We used to stop in here on the way home from work. It's gone all upmarket and fancy.'

'The same doctors still frequent it but they earn more so I guess the proprietor saw an opportunity and grabbed it.' Jack leaned back in his seat and twirled his icy bottle of beer between his hands. Those days they'd thought they'd be together for ever. Correction. He'd thought that. Ruby had always intended on moving on.

Ruby slouched down in her chair and an eloquent shiver rolled through her upper body. 'You wouldn't think it was snowing up in the hills after how sunny it was earlier at the beach. Weather forecasts are less reliable than having your tarot cards read.'

Jack spluttered. 'You get your cards read?'

'The only time I did I was told I had a great future ahead of me as a truck driver.' She rested her chin on one finger. 'Or was it *with* a truck driver? I probably should've asked for my money back.'

'I reckon.' Jack chuckled and relaxed further. He liked it when Ruby was being funny. 'Though you do call your vehicle a truck so maybe there's something in it.'

'Maybe.' She grinned.

Jack looked around the room, trying to ignore Ruby's delectable mouth and the warm feelings it engendered deep inside him. 'That open fire makes it nice and cosy in here.'

Ruby's bottle banged loudly on the tabletop. She straightened up, her cheeks colouring fast.

Instantly Jack knew what she was remembering. Nice and cosy. Something to do with a sheep-skin rug, a bottle of wine that she'd swapped for a lager, and nakedness. Heat blasted through him. Why did everything they talked about bring back its own special memory? Those seven months had been the best of his life. He must've been mad not to have gone with her to the States, even if he'd believed qualifying was the most impor-tant thing in his life. Hell, why hadn't he asked her to wait a few more months?

Because he'd been afraid she'd say no. Afraid to lay his heart on the line. Even more afraid than he'd been of being left alone. And because of his reticence she had gone, taking his heart with her.

It wasn't too late to rectify everything. He could stay here, not go off into the wild blue yonder. Except it wouldn't work. Getting involved with Ruby again meant living on a knife edge, always wondering if she'd still be lying beside him when he woke up in the morning, never knowing what might trigger her next disappearing act.

No, he couldn't do that. Not if he wanted to stay sane and remotely happy.

Huh, did he really think he could be at all happy

without her? Well, he'd find the answer to that soon enough. October was rapidly approaching and he'd be gone.

CHAPTER EIGHT

'JULIE, you're late. I hope you've got a good reason.' Jack raised his voice so he would be heard out on the tarmac where his office lady stood chatting to Ruby.

He saw Ruby give Julie a sympathetic look, heard her ask, 'What's up with him? You leave him too many letters to sign last night?'

As Jack's temper increased, Julie glanced nervously at him. 'Guess I'd better find out.'

'Isn't being late to work a good enough reason to call you out?' Jack growled at Julie as she approached.

Ruby followed, the packs slung over her shoulders. Her step was as jaunty as ever. Did nothing upset her these days?

'I'll be with you shortly.' He scowled at Ruby, before turning to Julie and dropping the level of his roar a decibel. Not enough if the way Julie flinched was anything to go by. 'Where have you been? I'd hoped to see the mail before I get called out.'

Julie stared up into his face, two red spots staining her cheeks, and said breathlessly, 'I don't officially start until nine. Most days I'm early because I drop the kids off at school and come straight on here. Today I had other things to do first.'

Jack started, gulped down his shock. 'I see.' Why hadn't he known that? He was such an idiot. All because he'd had a sleepless night trying to decide what to do when he returned from Scott Base. The idea of heading down south without definite plans for afterwards had begun eating at him, creating an urgency within him that he didn't know how to fix. The idea of wandering aimlessly to somewhere else was panicking him.

Julie rocked back on her heels. 'There isn't any mail today.' And she walked into her office.

Jack knew he was being watched and spun around to encounter Ruby's hot, angry gaze.

'What was that all about?' she demanded.

'I got something wrong, that's all.' *None of your business, Red. Ruby. Damn it. Ruby.*

'Then you'd better apologise to Julie.' Ruby

turned into the storeroom, dropping the bags onto the floor.

'Don't be so heavy-handed with those,' Jack bawled after her. 'Broken vials cost money to replace.'

Ruby slapped her hands on her hips, her chin tilted at a dangerous angle. 'You fall out of bed this morning? Or burn the toast, over-fry the eggs?'

All of the above. Because of his foul mood. He jammed rigid fingers through his hair. 'Damn it.' His long strides ate up the distance to his office. The door slammed, satisfyingly rattling the walls.

He stabbed the 'on' button of his laptop and paced back and forth across the tiny room until the desktop icons appeared. He'd be decisive. All this uncertainty was tearing him apart. Once he had a plan in place for the next twelve months he'd be able to cope with Ruby, would manage to keep her from getting under his skin and making him wish he could stay here with her.

He quickly found the folder labelled 'The Future' containing three job applications. Click, send. Click, send. Click, send. All three were on their way, whizzing through cyberspace. Surely he'd get something from one of them. Then he'd know what the hell he was doing.

Ruby waved up at Jack as he peered down from the helicopter. His foul mood was still bubbling between them, but right now he should get over it. They were on a job. 'Take the hook away,' she snapped into her mouthpiece before starting across the slippery boulders. She was heading to the man huddled against the rocks, sheltering from the spume coming off the sea. Another man lay sprawled beside him. The shattered hull of their boat rested upside down five metres away. Ruby shuddered. These men were incredibly lucky to be alive. According to the report that had come through to the helicopter, the driver of the boat had cut too close to the shoreline and crashed into submerged rocks.

A dented scallop dreg lay on a tangle of ropes. Ruby didn't know the exact quota for private fishermen but she'd bet there were hundreds more scallops strewn over the scene than these two were entitled to. Picking her way carefully, the pack heavy on her back, she called out, 'Hi, guys. I'm Ruby, a paramedic.'

'About time you showed up. Where the hell you been? Stop at the pub on the way, did ya?' Judging by the slurred words, he was the one who'd been drinking.

Ruby studied him carefully. Drinking and boating made a dangerous combination. Probably the reason for this predicament. But it wasn't her place to criticise. She was making a judgement call that could be very wrong. 'We came the moment we got the call. I guess it seemed like a lifetime, waiting for us to turn up.'

'You can cut the nice-girl stuff and get on with helping me. I reckon I've broken me arm.' His left arm was tucked against his chest.

Ruby walked past the belligerent man and approached his mate lying face up on the rocks. 'I'll be with you in a minute, sir. Your friend looks like he's unconscious.' Or deceased. Blood had pooled beside the man's head but no wound was obvious from this angle.

'I could've told you that. Doesn't take a rocket scientist to know he's out for the count. Why are you looking at him? He can't feel anything. My arm's hurting like hell.'

Ruby knelt beside the apparently unconscious man and searched for any signs of life, eventually finding a very weak carotid pulse. Speaking into her mouthpiece, Ruby told Jack, 'Need the stretcher, one collar and the backboard.'

'On the way.' Still terse.

'Hey, girlie, you listening to me at all?' The man loomed above her, reeking of fish and booze.

A flicker of concern washed over Ruby. Where was Jack? This man's menacing attitude made her uncomfortable. Plastering on the sweetest smile she could raise, she told him, 'I'll be with you shortly, sir. Can you tell me your names?'

'What's names matter? You should be fixing me up.' The slurring seemed worse.

'Do you remember how long ago you crashed?' For all she knew, this guy might've been knocked out too.

'I don't know. Hours ago.'

'Has your friend been unconscious all that time?'

'I guess. I dragged him away from the boat in case it went up in flames. The fuel went everywhere.' He tried to step closer, staggered and sank down on his rump. His injured arm banged onto his knees, and his roar of pain made Ruby cringe. His cussing was long and loud, turning the air blue.

'Sir, are you a diabetic?' she asked. He appeared to be about fifty and had a very rotund figure, a prime candidate for the disease. She needed to check his blood-sugar level. A raised result could explain his slurred speech. But there was no denying the strong smell of alcohol.

'No, I'm not. What's that got to do with me arm?' He managed to get back on his feet, swaying in all directions, his good arm raised at her.

Ruby held her breath, and kept her mouth shut. Saying anything at all would only crank his anger levels higher. Heck, she was surrounded by angry men. Finally, when this particular one didn't move towards her, she spoke quietly into her mouthpiece. 'What's keeping you, Jack? I've got a problem here. Alcohol involved. But not sure if he's had too much or if he has an insulin crisis.'

'Onto it.' Jack's voice, laced with fury, came through her earpiece. Like she needed his attitude right now. She had another patient desperately requiring attention. But as Ruby started towards the unconscious man a heavy hand grabbed her shoulder, flipped her round. Pain stabbed her bad knee as it twisted, and she couldn't hold in a groan.

'Leave him,' her tormenter snarled, his face only inches from hers. 'Deal with me first.'

Spittle covered his chin, big bloodshot eyes filled Ruby's vision, and the stench of sour alcohol made her nauseous as her stomach clenched in fright. For all his bulk he'd moved fast, surprising her from behind. What was this guy about? He wouldn't, couldn't, hurt her. Not when she was there to help. She opened her mouth to talk him down, but no words came out.

A fist came into sight to her left. She ducked. The man swayed on his feet, missed connecting with her, and she hurriedly stumbled backwards.

Jack could barely control his fury as he charged recklessly across the slippery rocks. If that idiot touched Ruby again there'd be no accounting for what he might do. When the maniac had grabbed Red, fear had gripped him, stopped his breathing. Stopped his heart. All the anger he'd been directing at himself for his appalling behaviour back at base was now focused on this man. What chance did tiny Ruby have if that guy took another swing at her and connected? She might act tough but she was minuscule against her assailant. Jack skidded, righted himself, charged ahead. He could see Ruby straightening up, shock turning to rage in her expressive face. *Don't, Red. Don't antagonise him. Play it safe. Go for quiet, calm. If anyone's going to knock his block off, I will.*

How could anyone in their right mind think of hurting Ruby? She was trying to help, for pity's sake. Jack stopped a metre from the man, sucked a breath, then another, and said, 'Hey, there, how are you doing, mate?'

The guy whipped around, stumbled and sat down hard again. The language that followed was colourful.

Jack reached out, touched Ruby's arm. 'You okay?'

Her eyes were large in her very pale face and she swallowed hard, but all she said was, 'What took you so long?' Then she headed to the other patient.

He stared after her, a grin beginning deep inside him, some of his fury abating. *You're one tough woman, Ruby Smith.* Then his grin stopped. She was limping again.

Dropping to his haunches in front of the problem patient, Jack bit down on a few sharp words and said, 'Got yourself into a bit of a pickle here, I see. I'm Jack, by the way. A doctor.'

That really focused the guy. 'So why'd you send the girlie down first, then, eh? I need a real doctor, not one of those poncy medics who think they know everything. She hasn't even looked at my arm, reckons me mate should be looked at first.' He started pushing up on his feet.

Jack shook his head at the guy's total lack of concern for his friend. 'Can you remain sitting, sir, while I take a wee drop of blood from your thumb?'

'What for? What kind of doctor are you? It's me arm you should be worried about, not me blood.'

'I want to check your sugar levels,' Jack reassured him. 'You're a bit wobbly on your feet.' Thank goodness or Ruby might now be lying stretched out on the rocks. He snapped open the glucometer case. *Calm down, Jacko. There's nothing to be gained by giving this idiot what for.* Except he'd feel a heap better. With a wry smile Jack quickly pricked the guy's thumb and placed a drop of blood on the tab for the meter to read.

Ruby grimaced. The rocks dug into her knees as she examined the unconscious man, taking his BP, pulse rate. A massive haematoma had formed above his left eye, but no other injuries were evident on the top side of his head. A pool of blood had congealed around the man's shoulder. Feeling through a slash in his heavy oilskin jacket her gloved fingers encountered soft, torn tissue. Further examination revealed many cuts, some bone deep, on the man's torso, arms, legs. There'd be internal crush injuries for sure. She slit the trousers and winced. A line of bruises ran directly below both knees. Was this where the boat had hit?

Ruby's nerve endings flared in sympathy. When his pal had dragged him out from under the boat, he'd caused further abrasions. If this man hadn't been unconscious before that move, he'd surely have passed out from pain then. She reached for her pack and the IV kit.

Jack crouched down beside her, his shoulder gently nudging hers in support. 'What have you found so far?'

Ruby quickly ran through her observations as she inserted the cannula and ran a line in. 'According to our friend over there, the boat landed on him. Any spinal injuries might've been made worse when he was dragged clear.' She explained about the leaking fuel.

'Since he's already been moved, let's get the collar on and stretcher him ASAP. We'll give him fluids once we're on board. The sooner we get him to hospital the better.'

Working together, the patient was soon ready to be winched aboard. Ruby glanced at their now subdued second patient. 'You hit him over the head with a rock?'

Jack grunted. 'Painkiller.'

'His blood sugar?'

'Slightly high, not the cause of his speech impediment.' Jack dragged out the last word.

'Why do some boaties drink when they're out here? Haven't they got any brains in their skulls?' Ruby checked her patient's harness again before nodding at the other man. 'Think he'll go easy in the winch bucket?'

'Only one way to find out.' Jack crossed to check on the man. 'How're you doing, mate?'

'Get me off this place, will you?' The man glanced around at the carnage. 'That boat was me pride and joy. More fun than the wife.' His gaze reached the scallops and his head jerked around. 'Reckon you got room in that helicopter to take me shellfish? I'll give you some.' A harsh, smoky laugh followed. 'Them fisheries officers won't be looking for me at the airport.'

'Come on, let's get you and your pal on board.' Jack ignored the man's protests and rising temper over not being able to take his catch with him.

Ruby muttered under her breath as she prepared to be winched up first, 'Maybe the wife would like us to leave him out here.'

'Ruby Smith, you wicked girl.' Jack smiled at her briefly.

'Just telling it as I see it.' But she turned her head away, smiling. She could do wicked if that was what turned Jack on. High heels, black fishnet stockings, one of those figure-hugging body suits all in lace.

Jack muttered, 'Let the guys know what's going on. Slats can help you if our pal gets stroppy.'

The depth of concern for her in Jack's eyes brought tears welling up. Just a short while ago he'd been angry with her. She was so mixed up that she didn't even answer.

They didn't make it back to base. Another call came through minutes after offloading the boaties. Jack read the screen in the cockpit. '"Hiker in the Tararua Ranges, male, thirty-four years old, suspected broken pelvis from falling down a ravine yesterday. Stat three."'

'He's probably hypothermic. It rained during the night.' Ruby spoke through the headphones. 'What was the low last night, Chris?'

'Four degrees in the city, but probably closer to zero in the ranges, with sleet higher up. Better hope our man had a survival blanket with him.'

'Surely if they're smart enough to carry an emergency locator beacon they'll have a blanket.' Jack peered through the window at the desolate hills coming into view below. 'A night out in the ranges in the middle of winter is not my idea of fun. They probably take that tasteless, dried food with them as well.'

'The food would be right up Ruby's alley.' Chris studied the transponder, ignoring the spluttering going on in their headsets from Ruby.

'Getting a signal yet?' Jack asked. Standing behind the pilots, he studied all the dials in front of him. Some he knew from flying the Tomahawk, most didn't make any sense at all. He did recognise the transponder but didn't know how it worked.

'Yep.' Chris pointed. 'That needle directs me to the spot, and hopefully we'll find a clear patch in the bush with our patient in the middle. If not the patient then his companion should be there, ready to lead you to the guy.'

Jack told him, 'According to the search and rescue boffins, there were three hikers altogether. When our man fell the other two shifted him to a flat area above the river. One person stayed and put their tent up over him, while the other hiked out to get help.'

'Why are we only now going out on retrieval if that's the case? We could've got to him before nightfall. The weather wasn't an issue yesterday.'

Jack understood Chris's frustration. 'The woman walking out for help got lost, then darkness fell and she had to wait for daybreak to find her way back to the track.'

'Trouble comes in threes.' Chris grimaced. 'Here's the next problem.'

'What's wrong?' Ruby's voice zapped Jack's brain.

For a brief moment he'd forgotten she was there. How had that happened? These past weeks had been all about Ruby. Working with Ruby. Walking the dog, attacking her kitchen floor, sharing a beer at the pub with the team—and Ruby. He hadn't had any respite when he'd gone to bed either. She followed him there—unfortunately only in his head—and when he finally did manage to drop off to sleep she crawled into his dreams.

Chris was talking. 'The wind has returned. By the way those beech trees are lying over, the gusts are very strong. I don't like your chances of being winched down at the moment, Ruby.'

If there was any danger involved then Ruby wasn't going down. No argument. Jack twisted around to face her. 'I'll go.'

Her chin shoved forward. 'Jack, it's my day for going down first.'

'I'm pulling rank.' And losing respect. 'Please, Red.'

Those green orbs glittered. 'Don't even go there,' she ground out through clenched teeth. 'I know what to do.'

Chris's calm voice interrupted. 'No one's going unless I think it safe enough. I'm not having anyone hanging on the end of the line when one of those gusts hits. We'll wait a bit and see what the wind does. If we're lucky it'll be a brief squall.'

Jack's heart plummeted. He couldn't imagine flying away, leaving behind an injured person. 'Do your best to get me down.'

'Pardon?' Ruby retorted.

'Us down.' Anything to placate her.

Chris told them, 'If we get a window of opportunity I want you prepared and ready to go. No mucking about. Load and go. If the tent's not packed and ready, leave it. If you get down and the wind returns, I'll have to leave you with the patient.'

Chris's professional attitude settled Jack. He'd been wrong to try and replace Ruby. It was her drop and he shouldn't be bringing in personal concerns while on a job. But he'd worry fit to burst the whole time she was on that wire. And still believe he should've gone.

Jack pushed through to the back. 'Get hooked, Red.' *And stop glaring at me. I know I called you Red but right now I'm more concerned about your health and safety than what the pilots might think of what I call you.* 'If you need me down there, call up.'

She knows that, you idiot. She's been doing this stuff for a lot longer than you have. But not with him there to worry about her. Which she'd absolutely hate. And charged emotions were unsafe in this environment.

Ruby stood up and quietly got ready, but after she'd clicked the hook in place she reached out and touched his shoulder.

Why? Thanking him for giving in? For caring? For *showing* he cared? Jack dredged up a smile. 'Look out for yourself, okay?' He knew full well she'd ignore him but he'd had to say it. Hadn't been able to stop himself.

'It's looking good.' Chris's voice sounded in his ear. 'I'm going round. Get ready.'

They pulled the door open and waited. Jack's heart thudded dully. His finger traced a line over her hand, felt her shiver. 'Go well, ruby red girl.'

Chris again. 'Okay, Ruby, I'm over the spot. The moment you're unhooked I'll back off until Jack's got the stretcher ready. Good luck.'

And Ruby was over the edge and dropping as rapidly as the winch allowed. A short gust of wind rattled things inside the 'copter and Jack watched, his heart thudding in his ears, as Ruby spun out of control on the end of the wire. Her slight body offered no resistance to the wind. Jack's teeth bit painfully into his bottom lip as she swung close to the top of a huge beech tree. His imagination drew a horrific picture of Red splattered against those thick branches.

The helicopter lifted quickly, taking Ruby out of harm's way. Then as suddenly as the wind came up it dropped and Chris was edging Ruby down to the ground.

Seconds later she was on her feet and unhitching the wire. 'Pull it up, Jack.' Her urgency came through the headset loud and clear. He responded instantly.

Ten minutes later he was bringing the laden

stretcher inside and lowering the hook again to retrieve Ruby and the other person on the ground.

'Phew. Well done, everyone,' Slats said as the 'copter rolled sideways and turned for home. 'That was a very fast turnaround.'

Jack focused on the patient and his broken pelvis, trying hard to quell the shaky feeling in his hands, the gnawing sensation in his gut. When that gust had caught Ruby he'd been utterly helpless to do anything for her. He, who always put himself out there for those he loved—cared deeply about—hadn't been able to do any more than watch. He'd been desperate to swap places with her. And now that she'd returned to the helicopter, safe and unscathed, he wanted to hold her tight and never let her go.

Like that was ever going to happen.

Ruby stretched her legs out straight, trying not to wince. That landing back on the Tararuas had been a little too hard, jarring her teeth and jolting her wonky knee. Coming on top of the twist it had received back at the boat-crash scene, her knee might take a bit of rest and relaxation to settle down this time. She seemed to have been giving it a few too many knocks lately.

Please don't let it be the start of the problems the doctor in San Francisco had warned her about. Arthritis would naturally set in as she got older but, hey, that was light years away. The doctor, a serious man who believed she should leave dangerous ambulance work to the men, had told her in no uncertain terms that too many bumps and she'd find herself in need of a knee replacement.

'Problem?' Jack asked. 'That's the second time you've rubbed your knee.'

'Chris didn't give me a lot of time to unhook myself.'

Her headphone crackled as Chris growled light-heartedly, 'Yeah, right, blame me, why don't you?'

'I've noticed you limping a few times. How did you damage it?' Jack wasn't easily deflected.

She sighed. 'Not through working on the helicopters, that's the truth.' The last thing she needed was Jack going all protective on her. Like he'd already done twice today. The first time with that drunk idiot had made her feel all soft and gooey inside, and had stopped her from doing something to the idiot she'd regret for the rest of her life.

But Jack had gone too far when he'd said he'd swap places with her on the winch up in the hills. He'd overstepped the boundaries. Boss or not. She was as capable as anyone on the base of doing the job under difficult circumstances. If Chris had said it was a no-go then she'd have accepted his advice. But to be told she couldn't do a drop because Jack was worried about her? That was wrong. It would show her up as a second-rate team member.

Silence descended between them, the whine of the rotors suddenly loud. Finally Jack tapped her knee. 'You going to tell me?'

Maybe if he heard the story he'd understand how capable of looking after herself she was. 'Some screwball on a drug high attacked me and my crew partner late one night in San Francisco when we were called to pick up a cardiac arrest at a house. He freaked us out by knocking on the windows while we were trying to resus our patient. When we carried the stretcher outside he held a knife to my partner's throat, demanding drugs.'

'Blimey, Red. What did you do?'

'I kind of kicked him to make him drop the weapon.'

'You kind of kicked him?' Jack's eyes were popping, his mouth twitching. 'Where it hurt the most?'

'Definitely.' She grinned. 'He wasn't happy and when he'd got his breath back he chased me out onto the road where I tripped, trying to dodge around a moving car. I went down hard, and had to have surgery, which put me on light duties for two months.'

'He didn't attack you again?'

'The car I was avoiding hit him.' The whole thing still gave her nightmares at times. 'By the time the drugs cleared out of his system he was in jail with a broken ankle.' She shuddered. 'It was all a bit freaky.'

'You ever go out on night calls again over there?'

'Not until I'd done a judo course.' Not easy with a dodgy knee but definitely good for the confidence levels when approaching drunks on the street late at night. But today when that boatie had swung at her, her training had seemed to evaporate and all she'd done had been to duck his arm.

Jack chuckled. 'That I'd pay to see. Tiny Ruby hoisting some big, uncooperative male over her shoulder. Remind me never to upset you again.' Then his smile faded. 'You restrained yourself today.'

Tiny Ruby? She conceded she only came up to Jack's chest. Had always tucked under his arm with room to spare. Glancing up, she found his gaze lingering on her and muttered distractedly, 'No, I blew it. Didn't react as I should've. I could do with some practice.'

'Want a partner? I've done a little tai kwon do.'

Ruby's pulse picked up speed. She and Jack on a mat, practising moves and throws? Up close and personal? Twisting their legs around each other. Pulling his body over her shoulder. Being pulled over his, their jackets sliding past each other. Her tongue began doing laps of her mouth.

The radio interrupted. 'Another call,' Jack muttered.

Ruby sighed with relief at her lucky escape

from having to answer his invitation. 'No rest for the wicked.' Why was wicked coming to mind so much today?

CHAPTER NINE

AT HOME Jack tossed his keys on the dining table and picked up the pile of mail Johnny must've collected. Idly flicking through the envelopes, he headed for a cold beer.

'Rates, car registration, Visa card bill.' He tossed those aside. Everyone wanted his money.

Pulling open the fridge, he snatched up a beer and butted the door closed with his hip. The last envelope in his hand was white with the Antarctica Project logo emblazoned across the bottom corner. Jack stared at it. He'd been waiting weeks for this, wondering if the boffins running the summer programme were ever going to make up their minds about staffing and finalise his contract.

Hooking out a stool with his foot, Jack sank down at the breakfast bar, turning the envelope over and over. And over. He twisted the top off his bottle and drained half the contents.

'Dr Jack Forbes,' he read. So here it was. The result of two interviews for the most amazing job on the planet. Summer down near the South Pole.

Open the damned thing. Sign the contract. And move forward. Jack dropped the envelope onto the counter. Looked around the ultra-modern kitchen and felt nothing. No pride in ownership. No sense of home. Merely a place to put his head down at night after a hard day at work. Nothing like Ruby's villa, full of character, filled with Ruby, her scent, her laughter, her presence. Yes, she had made a home for herself.

Tugging his wallet from his pocket, he found the photo he'd carried for three years. Long sherry-coloured hair flowed over Ruby's shoulders where his arm rested. Her sensual mouth had split into a wide grin and for once those beautiful eyes held no tension. He visualised the short black dress she'd worn that night, how it had fitted like a second skin—and teased him all evening. His gaze slid sideways and he studied himself. Happy, in love and totally out of his depth with the woman in his arms. No change, then.

He slapped the photo down. None of this had

anything to do with the letter in front of him. Draining the bottle, he reached into the fridge for another. And slit the envelope open, shook the letter out. Picking it up, he stared at the folded pages.

'Hey, buddy.' Johnny strolled into the kitchen, tugged open the fridge for a beer. 'How was your day?'

Jack set the letter aside. 'Busy, and dangerous.'

'See you got a letter about that summer job. What did they say?' Johnny plonked his butt on a stool at the other end of the bar.

'I was just getting to it.' Jack finally unfolded the letter. Read it with a sinking heart. 'Damn.'

'Aw, man, you didn't get the job? I thought it was already decided.'

'This is the contract.' Jack skimmed over the details. 'I leave from Christchurch on October twenty-first.'

'That's fantastic. You must be stoked. Let's go to the pub and celebrate.'

'No, think I'll stay in. Got a few things to do.' Like what?

His friend studied him over the top of his bottle. 'Aren't you meant to be jumping with excitement? You wanted this big time.'

'I still do.' *I think.*

'It's Ruby, isn't it? She's got to you again.'

After taking a swig, Jack banged his bottle down. 'Not at all. She has nothing to do with this. Nothing, do you hear? I do want to go to Scott Base. This is a once-in-a-lifetime opportunity. It'll be awesome down there.'

'The man protests too much,' Johnny said around the mouth of his bottle.

The problem was it was impossible to fool a close friend. 'Some pea-brain threatened her today. He was drunk and belligerent. Then...' Jack sucked air into his lungs. 'Then she had a hairy ride down to a patient in the middle of the bush.'

'And you not signing this contract...' Johnny stabbed the letter '...will help her how?'

Jack shivered. 'That's just it. It won't.' Ruby didn't need him there to hold her hand, protect her back, keep her safe. She managed perfectly well without him.

But could he manage without her in his life now? He'd begun looking forward to her ribbing him every day. She was there full of unwanted advice whenever they had a bad day on the job. His days off were spent doing fun things with her.

'Twelve weeks. Not a lot of time to be away.' Johnny's reasonable tone broke into Jack's rising panic. 'You'll be back before you know it and probably wishing you could stay down there for longer.'

'You're right.' Twelve weeks without Ruby in them. What had happened here? He'd been hoping for this job for so long and should be crazy with excitement.

'So that's a yes, then? You'll go?'

'I guess.' The break from Ruby might be for the best. He was becoming too fond of her again, spent too much time thinking about her. She was settled in that house of hers, with her crazy mutt and the kids over the road. Ruby didn't need him as he needed her.

There was the scary thing—admitting he needed her. But what to do about it? He and Ruby had fitted together well three years ago. Now that fit seemed to be growing more cohesive, more right. *Ruby's essential to you, Jacko. Yeah.* He shoved a hand through his hair. That was the problem. Ruby was his rock. Always had been, always would be.

So option one—he'd go away, put the distance between them. A shiver rocked him. He'd sent other applications that morning for jobs he could get seriously interested in. He might be about to embark on years of living away. Reaching for a pen, he quickly scrawled his signature across the contract and shoved it into the prepaid envelope. Sealed it.

Jack spun off his stool, snatched up his keys. 'Your offer of a trip to the pub still on, Johnny?'

'The twins were so cute. Even with all those tubes and things.' Ruby hugged herself as Jack parked his car outside her house on their next day off. The tiny girls looked utterly defenceless in their incubators, while Mary and Colin had been exhausted. 'Ruby and Jackie. How cute is that? No one's ever named their child after me before.'

'Not sure how I feel about Jackie.' Jack grinned.

'The girls will be all right, won't they? I'm sure they're a bit bigger than last time we visited.'

'Early days yet, Ruby. Their lungs need to

develop. Thirty-one weeks is very prem. You know that.'

'Yes, but—'

'It's a waiting game. They'll be monitored continuously.' Jack switched off the engine and turned to face her. The preoccupied look hovering in his eyes for days now was still there. 'We did a good job, rescuing them. Now it's up to the twins to fight for themselves.'

'I know.' Something like pain snagged Ruby. She'd hate it if something ever happened to her babies. She wanted babies now? When had that happened? *Get out of Jack's car and go and see Zane. He's your baby.* 'Want a coffee?'

Darn it. So much for keeping her mouth shut around Jack. Spending most of her days off with him was only frustrating her. She longed to hug him, kiss him, make love with him. She wanted to speed up the getting-to-know-him process. She'd got it bad.

Her gate was off its latch. A prickle of apprehension slid down her spine. 'Zane? Here, boy.'

She rounded the corner and stopped. Seated in a row on her back porch were Toby, Thomas and Tory. Their small faces were red and puffy, and tears had made tracks down their cheeks. In unison they looked up at her, then dropped their heads again. Sniff, sniff.

'What's up, guys?'

The boys shuffled closer together, almost sitting on top of each other.

Jack laid a hand on her shoulder, moved closer to her. 'Any guesses?'

Ruby looked around the yard. 'Zane?' No answering woof. No beloved dog bounding across the wet lawn to put his muddy paws on her shoulders. No ball pressed into her hand. Her heart started banging crazily, painfully, against her ribs. 'Where's Zane, boys?'

'We're really sorry, Ruby.' Toby.

'We meant to shut the gate.' Thomas.

'It's our fault.' Tory.

Ruby stared at the boys, her breath stuck in her lungs. 'Is Zane hurt?' Please say no. Please.

Three little heads nodded. Three noses sniffed. 'Dad's taken him to the vet,' Thomas whispered.

The vet? Fear clutched Ruby. Zane couldn't be injured. Could he? What had happened? Oh, no. Was he alive? Pain sliced through her as she struggled to remain calm. Zane had to be all right. He had to be.

Jack's arm slid around her waist, held her upright. 'Easy. We'll find out everything.'

'Mum said we had to wait here for you,' Thomas continued. 'Are you going to be angry with us?'

Leaning into Jack, Ruby tried to quell the panic tearing up her throat. *Be strong, be tough.* Glancing down at the boys again, she saw their fear, their guilt; and her heart went out to them. Whatever had happened, they were only little boys.

She dropped to her knees and spread her arms out to encircle them. Her hug was fierce, filled with fear for her pet and her need to let these kids know she still cared about them too. 'It's okay, boys. I'm sure you didn't mean anything bad to happen to Zane.' Leaning back so she could see their faces, she asked, 'Did you?'

Three heads swung left, then right, and back. 'No.'

'I knew you wouldn't. You all love Zane like I do.' Ruby forced patience into her voice while inside she was screaming out, *What happened?* 'Did you leave the gate open?'

'We didn't mean to.'

'Did Zane run out on the road?' she asked.

Three nods. 'A car came and ran over him.'

Her blood chilled. Ran over him? A sob broke from her throat. He might be big but he wouldn't withstand that. Her poor baby. At least the boys' father had taken him to the vet already. Another group hug and she stood up. 'You'd better go home and get warm, boys.'

Jack immediately put his arm around her again. 'Do you know which vet to go to?'

'I'll ask the boys' mother but I'm guessing the one at the bottom of the hill. That's where I take Zane for his vaccinations.'

With Jack holding her hand, they escorted the boys home and learned from a very embarrassed mother that Ruby had surmised correctly. Then Jack put Ruby back in his car and drove her to the veterinary clinic.

'Zane's being operated on,' Rod, the boys' father, told them when they arrived. 'His front left leg's broken and needs pinning.'

Ruby's mouth dried. When she tried to speak nothing came out. Her body began trembling. Tears welled up, dripped down her face.

Jack wrapped her in a hug, and asked over her head, 'Are there any other injuries?'

'I don't know,' Rod answered quietly. 'The vet took X-rays but he hasn't told me any more.'

A flicker of hope wove through the chill cramping Ruby. She squeezed her eyes shut and sent Zane a message. *Please be all right, my baby. Hang in there, for me, for you, Zany.*

'How were the boys?' Rod asked.

Jack answered, 'They've gone home. They did really well fronting up to Ruby.'

'Hopefully they'll have learnt something from this.' Rod ran a hand through his hair. 'I guess we're in for lots more trouble before they reach adulthood.'

Ruby managed a weak smile. 'Would you have them any other way?'

'Today? Most definitely.'

They all sat down in a corner and waited for an interminable amount of time. Ruby was frozen with terror. When at last a door behind Reception opened and a man swathed in blue theatre scrubs emerged, she was afraid to look at him in case she saw bad news in his eyes.

The vet crossed over to her. 'Ruby, Zane's going

to be fine. There's some bruising around his ribs and his broken leg. He'll have a limp to go with that blind eye but otherwise he's one very lucky dog.'

'Really? You're telling me the truth? There's nothing you're missing out?'

Jack interrupted with a crooked smile, 'Ruby and Zane, matching limps. I like it.'

Ruby batted him with the back of her hand. 'Thanks, pal.'

The vet smiled tiredly. 'Come through and see Zane for yourself while I explain what I've done. He's still out for the count but I understand you want to touch him and feel his chest rising and falling before you fully believe me.'

Ruby hesitated, turned to Rod. 'The boys will be relieved.'

'I'll go and tell them the good news.' Rod grimaced. 'And, Ruby? I'm sorry they went to see Zane while you were out.'

'Don't be. Boys and dogs. You can't stop them. I've always encouraged them to play with Zane.' Ruby took Jack's hand and tugged him into the operating room with her, still needing his support. So much for being strong and tough. The moment Jack was around she leaned on him. Everyone relied on Jack. Maybe they shouldn't. But he had never complained. If he had, would he be so restless now?

'Why are you so jittery?' Jack asked Ruby when they arrived back at her house. Her hands moved constantly on her thighs, her head turned left and right as she peered through the stormy night. She couldn't still be worried about Zane. She'd seen him, stroked his head until he'd have had a headache if he'd been awake, and knew his injuries weren't life-threatening.

Ruby shoved the door wide, hesitated. 'Do you want a beer?' There was a catch in her voice. 'Or a coffee? I can heat up something to eat.'

Realisation crashed through his brain. Ruby didn't want to be on her own. Because she was upset about Zane? Or didn't she like being in the house alone at night? Could be why she'd got a dog in the first place. 'A warm drink would go down a treat. I'm freezing.'

As Jack locked the car he thought back to when they'd lived together. No memories came to him of Ruby not wanting to be home alone. But then they'd shared the flat with others to save money so the chances were she'd never been by herself.

Inside she headed for her kitchen and plugged in the kettle. 'Can you light the fire for me? This house is colder than a freezer.'

'I'm onto it.' It was almost warmer outside in the icy wind.

When she passed him a mug of steaming coffee her hand shook. Jack's heart oozed love for her. He patted the couch beside him. 'Zane's going to be fine. It won't be long before he's dropping that raggedy old tennis ball at your feet and de-manding you toss it for him.'

'I know, but seeing him like that was horrible.' She plonked down heavily beside him, putting his coffee in jeopardy. 'My lively, never-sit-still boy knocked out and looking dead.' Big fat tears oozed out from the corners of her eyes, trailed down her pale cheeks and dripped off her chin.

Jack put his mug on the floor and wrapped an arm around her slight shoulders, gently tugged her closer. 'Zane is not going to die. The vet was adamant about that.'

'Knowing that and reliving the fear I felt when I first saw him are two different things. I'd be devastated if—' She trembled like a sparrow balancing in the wind.

'I know, Ruby, I know. You've really taken to this fella. He's your baby, isn't he?'

Against his chest her head nodded. 'I love him. He's so generous with his affection and all he wants in return is love, food and warmth.' She sagged a little closer. 'It feels like I'm being tested all the time. First the kitchen plans went awry, now Zane's been hurt. What's next?'

'Ever considered those are normal, everyday things that happen to people?'

'You think so?'

'I do.' He watched her sipping her coffee, her hands shaking.

Her gaze roamed the room, pausing at a photo of her mother, moving on to the water stain darkening the wallpaper above the door, to the worn patch in the carpet at the doorway where people had trodden for tens of years. 'There's so much to do,' she whispered. 'But I really want to achieve it all, put my mark on this place.'

The grief, the uncertainty, the angst seemed to slip out of her and she relaxed back against the couch. Not against him now. This was a Ruby he didn't know. Strong. Tough. For the first time since he'd met her years ago he believed she was happy within her space, comfortable in her own skin. That she liked the life she'd carved out for herself. Surprise rolled through him. Ruby had made it all happen despite the mixed-up, tormented girl she'd once been. Pride for her overlaid his surprise. Maybe this time she really wouldn't tear away somewhere else the moment life turned difficult.

Ruby said, 'I love this house. It's mine, and it has history for me. I don't know if I could leave, even if I wanted to. Which I don't.'

You left me, even when you apparently didn't want to.

'It wasn't easy, was it?' She turned deep green eyes onto him.

Had he spoken aloud? Or were his feelings so strong she'd read them in his face, felt them in the air? He'd left her too, remember? 'No.'

'Breaking up like we did, agreeing we each had very different paths to follow, it still hurt.' Her eyes darkened further. 'Sometimes, when it got really awful with my father, I wondered if I'd done the right thing.'

And? Don't leave him hanging. Tell him it had all been a big mistake. But then where would they go from here? Did he want to start again with her? Yes, if he could only take the risk. No, he was too restless to settle down now. Talk about ironic. 'We did what seemed right for both of us at the time. And we're different for it now.'

'You think?'

'I know. Look at Zane's accident. You were fantastic with the three Ts today.' The boys had been expecting a blasting from her. *He'd* been expecting her to react wildly. Instead she'd been so understanding and caring it had lanced his heart as she'd hauled the boys in for the hug they'd desperately needed. She'd make a brilliant mother one day. And that was something he shouldn't be thinking about. Kids? And Ruby? With Ruby? His heart crashed into his ribs. He was falling in love with her all over again. He wanted to be with Ruby for ever. Only this time he'd want the whole deal. House and kids. Dog and truck. With Ruby at his side.

He stood and crossed to sit on a chair. He had to maintain some semblance of control.

'The three Ts? Is that what you call the boys?'

Ruby's green orbs sparkled and her beautiful, full lips twitched with suppressed laughter, totally unaware of what was going on in his mind. 'The three Ts. I like it.'

She'd ignored his compliment about how she'd handled the boys. The Ruby of old wouldn't have. She'd have taken it and analysed it until it no longer meant anything. She'd been so unable to believe a good thing about herself back then.

Now she scrambled to her feet. 'I'll put a casserole in the oven to heat. I'm starving.'

'When aren't you? That's something that hasn't changed about you. Where do you put all the food you manage to swallow?' He could do everyday conversation. Just.

'One day, when I'm fifty, I'll balloon into something the size of a house and you'll be able to say you told me so.' She spun out of the room, leaving him staring after her.

As if he would be around in twenty-four years' time to know what had happened to her. That thought saddened him. Now that he'd found Ruby again, he didn't want to lose touch. He cared what happened to her. Which reminded him…

Following her into the bright, shiny new

kitchen, he leaned against the cupboards and asked, 'Are you okay, being here at night without Zane?'

The spoon she was stirring the casserole with clattered against the dish. 'Why wouldn't I be?'

'Because if you aren't, I can sleep on the couch.'

'You're a bit long for that old lumpy thing.'

'There's the spare bedroom, though it's probably cold enough to freeze my lungs. Steve and Johnny won't miss me. They're going to a party tonight.' One he should be attending too. The guys would give him grief tomorrow when he explained he'd been with Ruby.

Ruby was stirring the life out of their dinner. 'If you don't want to go home, that's fine by me.'

'Where are the sheets? I'll go make up the bed now, and leave the door open so some warm air has a chance to make its way down the hall and inside the room.'

'Linen cupboard's next to the spare room.' Ruby put down the spoon and lifted the dish into the oven. Her shoulders relaxed and she began humming.

Jack grinned. She'd never admit she was glad to have someone in the house with her overnight. Where had this fear of the night come from? It didn't matter. He'd see she was okay. He should've told her he'd be better placed to protect her if he slept in her bedroom.

His grin slipped. As if he'd be sleeping then. Face it, he wasn't going to get much sleep just being in the same house as her. He shouldn't have offered to stay. Toughen up. One night. He'd manage.

Hell, what if Zane didn't come home tomorrow?

CHAPTER TEN

RUBY sat upright. A loud crack had snatched her out of the cosy dreamlike state she'd succumbed to. What was that noise? Wind rattled her windows, rain pelted the glass. Everywhere was black. No hall light. The green numbers of her bedside clock were gone. Blood pounded in her ears. What had happened? Had someone deliberately turned off her power?

Crack.

She jerked around, stared through the pitch dark at where the window should be. Someone was out there. Why wasn't Zane barking? Duh. Zane was at the vet clinic. So where was Jack? He was supposed to be looking out for her. 'Jack?'

'I'm here, Ruby. You okay?'

Crack.

'No, I'm not. There're no lights anywhere. And what's…?' she hiccuped. How embarrassing.

'What's that loud creaking sound?' Yikes, now her voice sounded like a screeching soprano's.

Her bed rocked. 'Can't see a thing,' Jack growled in the dark.

If she hadn't been in such a panic his sexy voice would've had her scrambling to haul him under the sheets with her. Great cure for panic. She moved and reached out in the dark for him. The bed moved sideways, tipping her backwards. 'What are you doing?'

'Trying to reach you.'

'I'm on the bed.'

'Yes, Ruby, I got that.' A warm hand touched her leg. 'If this isn't you then I'm in big trouble.'

He sounded too darned chirpy. She was freaking out. 'You're okay, it's me.' And think what she liked, his hand on her knee felt right. The thumping in her ears slowed, quietened. Replaced by a steady crashing in her chest.

'Have you got a torch handy? The power must have gone out. All the streetlights are out too.' His hand made it up to her arm.

Jack's practicality steadied her, even her fickle heart. 'In the top drawer of my bedside cabinet.' She rummaged around in the dark, finally finding the torch. 'Note to self, leave torch on top of cabinet in future.' Jack's welcome face sprang out of the dark as she flicked the beam on. 'Hi.'

'Hi, yourself. Let's go and get that fire roaring. That'll give us light and warmth. We could drag your mattress into the lounge, put it in front of the fire and be really snug.'

Gulp. Snug with Jack. Sounded too good to be true.

Creeeeak. Crack. Crash.

The house jolted, rocked. The sound of breaking glass could be heard over the other noises.

Ruby jumped. 'What was that?'

Jack reached for her hand and stood up. 'Let's find out. Could be the wind's coming from a different direction than usual and causing trees to scrape against the house.'

'That wouldn't make the house shake, though. It wasn't an earthquake, was it?'

'Definitely not.'

She waved the torch around, feeling better as familiar things sprang into sight. She tightened her grip on Jack's hand. His warmth helped enormously to banish the chill inside her; his strength gave her strength.

'Oh.' Ruby stared at the devastation before her when they stepped out onto the porch. The huge walnut tree lay twisted and broken, filling her yard with its massive branches. Her torch high-lighted the wooden fence now broken where a large branch had crashed on it. 'My beautiful walnut tree.' The torn trunk loomed eerily out of the dark. 'I loved that tree. Granddad hung a swing off it for me when I was little.' Sadness twisted through her gut.

'Your grandfather lived here?' Jack gaped at her.

She nodded slowly, before directing the torch at her laundry room. 'There's the explanation for the breaking glass.' A branch had pushed through the window. 'Lucky Zane isn't in there tonight.' A gust of wind slammed into her, forcing her back a step. She tugged her top tighter around her neck. The air was arctic.

Jack ordered, 'Direct the torch onto the fence. I want to see if the tree has hit Mrs Crocombe's place.'

'She's gone to stay with a friend for the week-end.' Thank goodness, or else she'd have been terrified when the tree came down.

'Looks all right from here,' Jack said. 'Let's get that fire cranked up. There's nothing you can do outside until the morning.' Jack's voice was so reasonable it angered her.

'Sure.' She slammed the door shut behind them. 'What's up?'

'Do you really have to ask?' Ruby leaned back against the door. What was he blind? 'How do I clear away all that huge tree? My vegetable garden is under those branches, all my plants no doubt squashed out of recognition. Did I mention my laundry now has a gaping hole where the window used to be? More work, more money.' Tears pricked the backs of her eyelids. Her hands balled into fists. 'It's never-ending. It's like something out there wants me gone.'

Jack's arm draped across her shoulders. 'Come on, you'll get through this. You're strong. If you want something badly enough, I know you'll make it happen.' He led her into the kitchen. 'Have you got another torch? I've changed my mind. I will go outside and check on the house.'

Dragging her shivering body away from his warmth, Ruby tugged a drawer open and withdrew a box of candles. 'I'll light some of these so you can take the torch.' He thought she was strong. If only he knew how much she depended on having him nearby to boost her confidence.

When Jack headed outside she couldn't hold in her despair any longer. Her fists banged the bench time and again. Her frustration erupted. 'Why pick on me?' Thump, thump. 'What have I done to deserve this? I want to establish my home, not have to fight for every step of the way.' Her hands ached with the pounding they were getting on the granite bench.

'Hey, take it easy.' Jack stepped up beside her. 'What's this all about?'

'I was looking forward to collecting walnuts for years to come.' Even hanging a swing for those kids she'd started thinking she might have one day.

'I'll buy you a new one. Not quite the same, I know, but it will be with you for years, while that old one was going to have to come down some time soon.'

'It'll be ages before I get the yard cleared enough to plant another tree.' Or made her vegetable patch workable again. But she mustn't give up on her dream. *Be tough, be strong.* She'd taken two hits today. Tomorrow was another day. Hopefully a darned sight better one.

Jack started towards the lounge. 'Let's make the place a bit warmer. And you can tell me how you came to be living in the house your grandfather used to own.'

She trailed after him, slightly ashamed of her outburst. 'When it came on the market, the lawyer looking after Mum's estate emailed me in the States and I had to have it. I'd have paid twice the price if necessary.'

'Back up. Did your grandfather live here when you were in Wellington with me?'

'No, he died when I was ten. Mum occasionally brought me to visit when I was little but they didn't get on very well because of how Mum was always on the move. Granddad said it wasn't the right way to bring me up and they had a big fight about that.' Ruby automatically flicked on the light switch as she moved into the lounge. 'Duh, stupid,' she muttered.

'You? Or your mum?'

Her mind was whirling. 'You know something? I always figured I moved a lot because I needed to find my father, but did I learn the habit from Mum?'

'I suppose if you've never stopped in one place for long you wouldn't know what it's like. And yet you're managing it now.' Jack moved the couch back to make room for her double-sized mattress.

Shock jolted Ruby. 'You're starting to believe me?'

'I got it loud and clear when you mentioned the swing your grandfather made for you in that tree.' His smile was endearingly crooked. 'I finally understand how much this place means to you.' Jack wrapped her in his arms. 'You're here to stay.'

'For ever.' If only that included being in Jack's arms for ever. But despite getting to know each other again he obviously didn't feel she could provide what he needed. Slowly stretching up on her toes, Ruby placed a soft kiss on his cheek, restraining from giving him the full-blown lips-to-lips kiss she ached for. She whispered, 'For ever.' She'd wait for him anyway. She had no choice.

Sliding down his body, she stepped away from

those strong, supportive arms, and went in search of blankets and pillows.

Jack awkwardly manoeuvred the mattress and dropped it in front of the fire, sending a gush of flame-laden air up the chimney. 'That's heavy.'

Ruby rolled herself into one of the blankets before nodding to the other. 'Here, tuck that around you to keep the draughts out.' She'd keep temptation at bay with her arms pinned in the cocoon.

Jack smiled as he did as he was told. 'Sure you'll be warm enough? I mean, you had about fifty blankets on your bed, now you've got one.'

'But it's wrapped around me more than once. I probably look like an Egyptian mummy.' Lying down on the side closest to the fire, she cracked a grin. 'Besides, I've got the best place. Those flames will keep me cosy.' There was that word again. Cosy. Like snug, it made her want to curl up against Jack and slide her arms around his warm, muscular body, bury her face against his chest and pretend this was how they always spent their evenings.

Rolling onto her back, she stared at Jack, suddenly remembering other nights lying in front of a fire together. Nights of passion. Nights when she'd believed she had it all, hadn't understood how easy it would be to lose everything, everyone, she cared about. The flickering flames cast shadows over the firm planes of Jack's face. Tugging an arm free, she ran her palm over his cheek, his chin, felt the light rasp of the beginning of whiskers.

Jack turned his head slightly so his lips were on her palm. He kissed her hand. He stroked her hot skin with his tongue. A tremor rippled down her arm. Followed by another. And another.

He laid his hand over hers. Desire rolled through her as she swam in the long-forgotten sensations swamping her. His eyes closed as he sank down closer to her, still stroking the palm of her hand. Such a small action, such a huge response. Ruby arched her back, squeezed her leg muscles tight as the sweet, hot desire continued rolling through her, building, building, building.

And then Jack was lying beside her, so close it was as though he was a part of her. Somehow he unwound her blanket and their bodies meshed, legs tangled, chest pressed to breasts, hips to hips, arms holding each other closer and closer.

Warmth became heat. So hot they were about to combust.

Light flooded the dark.

Ruby jerked, pulled back, blinking. 'I left that switch on.' She checked out the room. It looked normal, while she felt totally abnormal. Out of sorts. About to make love with Jack. Had the light saved them from making a mistake? Jack looked startled, then relieved. Acute disappointment flared in her tummy. So he wasn't really ready to get too close to her, and certainly not for the lovemaking that went with the kind of deep, meaningful relationship she wanted.

His beautiful eyes locked with hers, the glazed look slowly disappearing. He had wanted her. She'd felt it in his hands caressing her, his lips devouring hers, the sharpening of his muscles under her touch.

Ruby put space between them as she studied him. She wasn't about to throw herself at him, had to protect her pride. His mouth was swollen from their kisses. To have been tasting Jack after all this time had been wonderful. And was never going to happen again if the look now filtering into his eyes was anything to go by.

'Ruby?' Her name croaked off his tongue.

Funny that it hurt now he'd got used to calling her by her proper name. Every time he'd used Red it had given her hope, despite her ranting at him to use Ruby in front of others. A tiny piece of her believed that as long as he used the old affectionate name they'd had a chance of returning to their previous loving relationship. Now she understood there was no going back, only forward. What she needed to know was if Jack would ever come with her on that journey, but tonight wasn't the night to be asking.

Pulling further away, she got up and put another piece of wood on the fire. The raging heat of passion of moments ago had gone. If the power hadn't come on for a few more minutes they'd have been down and naked, and then there'd have been no stopping her. Sadness and a sense of loss gripped her. She didn't know if she was coming or going with Jack. 'I think we should go to sleep now.'

'You're right.' His words snapped through the air.

Behind her he tucked himself up and settled

on the far side of the mattress, not touching her at all.

The fire crackled and hissed as it devoured pine cuttings. Ruby watched the red-and-yellow flames dancing before her. So pretty, so dangerous. Was everything in life like that? Good and bad in every situation? As with Jack, being with him was wonderful, but every minute in his company put a strain on her heart, on her determination to leave him free to pursue his dreams. The dreams that would soon take him away from her.

'You've all got visitors.' Julie met Crew One as they disembarked after carrying an MVA victim to hospital the following week.

'We have? Who?' Jack asked as he handed down the pack to Ruby.

'It's a surprise, okay?' Julie looked smug.

Perplexed, Jack followed Julie inside. As station manager he'd have thought he'd be told prior to any one coming on base. 'Any ideas?' he asked Ruby.

She shrugged. 'Could be anybody.'

Stepping into the tearoom, Jack stopped at the sight of Lily Byrne and her parents sitting at the table, looking happy and, more importantly, healthy. At least Lily did. Her mother still wore a cast on her leg. 'This is a nice surprise.'

'We made you a cake,' Lily told him shyly.

Jack's heart lurched at the sight of the little girl. She was so cute with her shaven head now covered with a light growth of blonde hair. He hunkered down to her level. 'I love cake. How's your head?'

Lily smiled at him. 'It hurts sometimes and I cry but Daddy says it will stop soon.'

'I am very glad.' Jack straightened up and shook hands with Lily's parents. He didn't ask the questions raging around his head about the child's outcome. It wasn't his place. She looked fine, though he knew how deceptive that could be. Behind him he could feel Ruby pushing past. She immediately knelt down with Lily, chattering to her about the ballerinas printed on her pink dress.

Mrs Byrne spoke up, her eyes bright and glittery. 'Lily's going to be absolutely fine. The doctors don't expect any long-term effects from her injuries.'

Relief poured through Jack. A happy outcome.

Yes. This was why he did his job, for the good days. 'That's fantastic. And your leg?'

'Netball is off the programme for the rest of the season.' Lily's mother smiled softly. 'But that's so unimportant compared to getting Lily back to normal. I'd have broken both legs, if I'd had to, to save her.'

'Which is why we're here.' Mr Byrne placed a hand on his wife's shoulder. 'We wanted to thank you all for picking up Lily that day. Without the helicopter she'd have been a lot longer without the right treatment and the outcome might've been very different.'

Jack dipped his head at their pilot. 'Chris and Slats are the men you've got to thank for that.'

Chris shook hands with both parents. 'It's a team effort. I've got the easy job. Jack and Ruby here do the real work.'

'The doctors told us that you'd all helped to save Lily's life. When she had those fits she could've choked if you hadn't been there.'

Jack felt their anguish, as he had the day they'd lifted Lily off the road. He'd known it deep down as they'd flown to hospital, helping Lily fight for her life. He'd dreaded the outcome going the other way and these parents suffering as his had when Beth had died. He said gruffly, 'I'm thrilled we were in time.'

Ruby shook hands with the parents too, then grinned. 'Who's for coffee? That cake is begging to be eaten. Lily, what flavour is it?'

'Chocolate.' The little girl peered over the table. 'Do I have to have coffee too?'

Ruby clapped her hands. 'I'll find you some juice. And thank you for making my favourite cake. I love chocolate.'

'Me too.' The girl followed Ruby to the cupboard for a glass and then to the fridge for the juice. She stood by Ruby as she put the kettle on and spooned coffee granules into mugs. She got the milk out when Ruby asked her.

Jack waved everyone to a seat. Inside he felt warm, happy, as he watched Ruby with her little shadow. Ruby looked happy. She really had found her place in life and didn't need to go out in search of anything any more. His heart flipped. He thought of the job applications he'd started hearing back about. Emergency Specialist positions in Australia, England and on the African continent. Every week he added more advertisements to his file, and every week he deleted the expired ones. Apart from that day when he'd sent off three applications, he'd done nothing about seriously getting work for next year once he'd finished in the Antarctic. Something held him back from putting words down, prevented him posting his CV away. Something or someone?

Ruby?

When the family finally left, and with no call-out to take his mind off whatever was bothering him, Jack headed for his office to tackle the stack of mail Julie had left on his desk.

And to check his inbox for any new job ads.

'Okay, so who's going to the ball?' Jack tossed the invitations on the staffroom table a short time later.

'What ball?' Ruby reached for the pamphlet that lay under the invitations.

Chris stretched his legs under the table and leaned back in his chair. 'It's organised by our charity trust to raise money for the Rescue Helicopter base. We're all expected to go.'

'All of us? Think I'll be washing my hair that

night.' Ruby grinned. 'Can you imagine me all togged up in heels and a dress? Dancing?'

Jack nodded at her. 'Yes, I can. Remember that dinner-dance night we went to for the Wellington Hospital doctors? Correct me if I'm wrong, but you wore a dress that night.'

Heat spread across Ruby's cheeks. She'd worn a very short black dress with a low-cut neckline that had left little to the imagination. Her sherry-coloured hair had swirled around her, touching her waist, sliding across Jack's hands. He'd been stunned when he'd first set eyes on her that night. He hadn't recovered all evening, desperate to get away and take her to bed. 'That was back when I was young and fearless.' Or stupid. If she had to wear a dress this time, it would be something more subdued.

'You can't wear your overalls and boots.' Chris laughed.

'And you are going. With me. I'll make sure you don't renege.' Jack sauntered out to his office.

Ruby stared after him. 'What happened to asking nicely?'

Jack looked back over his shoulder. 'You'd have said no.'

'Of course I would've.' She couldn't go to the ball. Her? With Jack? They weren't dating. No, just lying together in front of the fire and getting as frustrated as it was possible to get.

Chris began texting on his phone. 'I'm letting Sandra know about it. When is the ball?'

'Three weeks' time. It's short notice but I think they've been selling tickets for a while now,' Jack called out.

'Typical. We're the last to find out anything and we're expected to turn up.' Ruby rinsed her cup. A bubble of excitement moved through her. A real ball. Dancing with Jack. Maybe she could find an exciting dress. It didn't have to be as provocative as that other one. She'd buy gorgeous shoes, new make-up and get her hair done. She shook her head. The hair thing might have to take a miss. Not enough to do anything glamorous with. Just because she usually wore jeans or jumpsuits it didn't mean she didn't love dressing up. She turned to Chris. 'What will Sandra think about this?'

'She'll love it. We had a great time last year, and everyone danced themselves to exhaustion. Seriously, Ruby, you'll enjoy it.' Then Chris's face fell. 'Whoops, better check the roster first. Just our luck we're on that night.'

They weren't. And later, when Jack told them he'd arranged for a crew from Nelson to come over and cover so that no one missed out, Ruby's excitement began to grow. This could be fun. She texted Sandra. 'Want 2 go dress shopping?'

Sandra replied instantly. 'Sat am. Pick u up 9.'

That night Ruby studied her meagre wardrobe. Forget ball dress, she really didn't have that many clothes full stop. When had she last bought something new? Some time in San Francisco. And because she hadn't been dating anyone there, her clothes had tended to be practical, not designed for fun.

She'd definitely splash out. Shoes were a priority. Her work boots, runners and sneakers didn't cut it for a ball. Roll on Saturday. There'd be some more serious damage done to her bank account. After the vet bills, paying for the laundry window to be reglazed and replacing some of the planks in the fence, her account looked a little sick. Thankfully Chris and the guys had all pitched in with chainsaws to cut up the fallen tree, while she and Sandra stacked the wood behind the house to dry for next winter's fires. But she might have to put that new lounge suite on hold for a while.

She shrugged. She couldn't wear a lounge suite. Couldn't wow Jack with one of those. And wow Jack she would.

'There's ice in that rain,' Ruby muttered, zipping her jacket collar as high as her throat allowed. 'Half an hour to go until I'm out of here. A hot roast at the pub for dinner tonight, I reckon.'

Chris growled, 'Now you've jinxed it for sure. No calls for three hours and I'll bet you that dinner we'll get one in the next few minutes.'

Someone's pager sounded loud and shrill. 'Darn,' Chris muttered. 'Didn't even get time to shake on the bet.'

Ruby and the men scrambled to their feet. Jack read his pager. 'Fisherman on a trawler twenty kilometres off the coast. Injured in the chest by a flying winch.'

Chris touched the computer screen, brought up the met forecast for the area they were about to head for. 'Marginal. There's every possibility that once I put you on board I'll have to leave you there until there's a break in the weather. It's the wind that's the problem.'

Jack rolled his eyes. 'Wonderful. But at least we'll be able to make the seaman comfortable. Hope the guy hasn't broken his ribs and punctured a lung.'

Ruby swallowed. 'Do they have roast meals on the trawler?' Not that she'd be eating one. She headed for her locker and retrieved a small bottle of seasickness tablets just in case she did end up staying on board.

'Got a spare one of those?' Jack asked from behind her.

She spun around. 'You get seasick too? You never mentioned that when we went out to the ferry on your first day.'

'I didn't get a chance. We were up and away so fast I had to hope we'd be as quick on board the ship.' He took the bottle of tablets she held out to him. 'Like you, I get motion sickness only at sea.'

'Let's hope this is a fast turnaround, then. Wouldn't look good for both of us to be puking over the side when we've got a patient to deal with.' She shoved the bottle at the back of her locker.

'You dropped something.' Jack bent down and stilled. 'You've still got this photo. That was taken at the doctors' dinner-dance.'

Ruby's cheeks warmed. She snatched the photo from his fingers. 'It's my favourite.'

Straightening, Jack pulled his wallet from his back pocket and flipped it open. 'Snap.'

Stunned, she stared at him. 'You kept a photo of us? Together.'

He shrugged. 'You kept a photo of us. Together.'

Her throat ached when she swallowed. Wow. What did this mean? Tucking her copy in her locker, she slammed the door and locked it. Peering up at Jack through her eyelashes, she found him watching her with the same question in his eyes.

He smiled. 'Wow.'

Chris yelled, 'You two coming?'

The flight was bumpy. Every time Ruby glanced at Jack he was staring at her. Because of those photos? That dinner-dance? She thought about the upcoming ball and her dress. Excitement sizzled through her veins. She'd completely got over not wanting to go, could barely wait for the night to arrive. What would Jack say when he saw her all dressed up? Would his eyes go all glittery and bright shiny grey? Would he hold her close, really, really close? Bring it on. She was going to make a statement.

Chris's voice interrupted her glee. 'Here we go. The wind's quieter out here so let's make this a quick and safe turnaround.'

Ruby peered over the edge as Jack was lowered to the heaving deck below. Three crew members stood ready to help him the moment his feet touched down. Then Ruby joined Jack and they were led below decks to the sickbay, moving awkwardly along the narrow corridors of the rolling ship.

It was ten o'clock before Slats put the 'copter down on the tarmac back at base. 'Home, sweet home,' he drawled.

'So much for my roast.' Ruby shoved the door open and reached for a pack. 'Not that my stomach is too keen on that idea any more.'

'You still feel nauseous?' Jack placed the second bag beside hers.

'Settling down. But that was the worst I've ever felt. I'm glad we didn't have to stay on board overnight.' She dropped to the ground. Pain jagged her knee, and she gasped.

'Ruby? You okay?' Jack landed beside her.

'Sure.' Her teeth bit hard into her bottom lip as she waited for the pain to pass. Why hadn't she used the step? She'd already tweaked the knee landing on the trawler's deck. And it had been so good over the weeks since picking up that hiker.

'Let me take that bag.' Jack slung both packs over his shoulder and took her elbow.

She pulled away. 'I'm fine. I don't need mollycoddling.' But the pain wasn't diminishing as quickly as usual, and she hobbled cautiously towards the hangar.

'Don't be stubborn, Ruby. No one's going to think less of you because you've got a damaged knee.' Jack took her elbow again.

No one but me. 'My knee's fine.'

'You seen your doctor about it lately?'

'I get regular check-ups.' The last one had been when she'd first arrived back in Wellington, more than four months ago now. She couldn't take time off every time it hurt. She'd never be at work.

'When's the next one?'

Resisting the urge to spin around in front of

him and poke a finger in his chest, Ruby snarled, 'Drop it, Jack. I know what I'm doing.'

I'm protecting my job, the job I love more than any other I've had. The job that's a part of the new life I'm putting together. I can't risk losing it, not when the house keeps tossing up unpleasant and costly surprises, not when Zane is hurt. What if I did get grounded? What would I do then? I'm not leaving Wellington, that's for sure.

Really? asked a voice in her head. A voice she recognised as the one that had so often sent her packing and moving on.

'Really,' she snapped, clenching her jaw. 'Really.'

CHAPTER ELEVEN

JACK strolled into the conference hall, which had been decked out in red for the ball. Red, the colour of their helicopters. Red, the colour of Ruby's hair. Red, the girl who'd got to him again, knocked down his defences when he wasn't looking. He scanned the crowded tables, searching out his colleagues.

Looking for Red.

She'd managed to wriggle out of coming with him. Something to do with being late finishing at the hair salon. How long did it take to fix stunted hair? Ruby and Sandra had got ready together, at Chris's place. Ruby doing girl things with Sandra was nice. She'd not had a lot of that in the past.

Jack scanned the room for brilliant red hair. Surely that traffic-light colour had to stand out even in this crowd?

He found Chris first. He was standing at a table with a beer in his hand and talking to Slats, who looked distinctly uncomfortable. Jack started heading towards the pilots, constantly looking for Red.

Pow. A punch to the ribs. He jerked to a stop. And stared. What the hell had happened? Ruby stood on Chris's other side. Ruby in a black dress. *The* black dress. The one that she'd worn to the doctors' dinner-dance. The one that had taken his breath away back then. No air was drawing into his lungs now either. His feet were stuck to the floor as he stared at the beautiful apparition before him. The dress appeared to be painted on that splendid body. Just like last time. Except tonight she wore a wide red belt cinched at her narrow waist.

Ruby in a dress. His gaze trailed downwards and a surge of laughter rolled through him. Ruby's shoes were an exact match for her belt, with heels about a metre high. How did she balance up there? Could she breathe the rarefied air? As for dancing on those things—impossible.

'Hey, Jack.' Ruby waved to him.

'Great to see ya, ruby-red girl,' he whispered, and began pressing forward again, his eyes glued to her. How had he, even for a fraction of a second, believed he'd got over Red?

Not only did he want to haul her into his arms and ravage her right here, right now, but he wanted to be around so he could hold her through all the ups and downs. He craved her body, her laughter and teasing, her loyalty, everything about her. He wanted to share his life with her.

Hell, a simple black dress had slammed him between the eyes, woken him up to what had been right before him all along. He smiled at her, his heart stuttering with love.

She blew him a kiss and gave a big, knowing wink.

Jack elbowed people out of his way and reached Ruby. Startled, he gaped at her. How had he missed that? 'Your hair.' That glittering red had vanished. It was coloured as close to her natural sherry gold shades as possible. His heart pumped hard. His mouth dried. The little minx. Red was setting her sights on him. He lifted his hands in surrender. He was all hers.

'Hey, Jack, isn't this awesome?' Ruby stood before him, grinning, her face a lot closer to his than usual thanks to those shoes. There was a cheeky twinkle in her eyes, a *knowing*, cheeky twinkle.

'Your hair. It looks fantastic.' Even cut so short, the colour brought back undimmed memories of running his hands through the silky layers. He groaned. This was going to be one heck of a night. Just keeping his hands to himself would be next to impossible. So why try?

'Let's dance.' He scooped her into his arms and glided across the floor. 'I hope you remember how much we danced last time you wore that dress.' Looking down, he saw her eyes widen, and heat flush up her neck endearingly. He ran a finger down her cheek. 'Because tonight we ain't going to stop, lady.'

And who knew where that would lead? At the dance three years ago they'd finished the night making love. Tonight? Who knew? But he had a damned good idea.

Ruby flopped down onto a chair, a brimming plate of food in front of her. But it was the cold drink she went for first. 'That's divine. It's so hot in here.'

Jack grinned back at her. 'Can't keep up?'

If she hadn't noticed the thin veneer of sweat on his brow she'd have thought Jack had been training for weeks. 'I can match you every dance step of the way.' Glug, glug. The cool water was heavenly in her throat. If only she could ignore the throbbing in her knee.

'That's good. There's plenty more where those last moves came from.' Jack sat down beside her, his suit jacket draped over the back of his chair.

'I'm up for anything once I've eaten this delicious-looking food.' She had to replenish her energy levels somehow. And give her leg a break.

Jack leaned close and whispered, 'Anything?'

'Anything on the dance floor.'

'Retracting your statement?' He winked.

'Just clarifying it.'

Sandra sat down on Ruby's other side, dabbing her eyes. 'I haven't had a night like this in ages.'

Ruby laughed, glad of the break from Jack's all-seeing eyes and double-edged banter, which she was rapidly losing control over. If she'd ever had any control.

Sandra leaned closer. 'Your Jack's a smooth mover.'

Her Jack? Since when had the base staff decided that? 'He seems to know what he's doing.'

Pine scent wafted past her nose. 'You bet I do,' the man himself whispered beside her ear.

Gulp. This really had to stop. Right here. Right now. But hadn't she set out to wow him? Didn't she want him in her bed tonight? Of course she did. So stop being coy. Pushing aside her barely touched plate, she grabbed for Jack's hand. 'Let's dance.'

'Red, I'm starving.' He blinked at her.

'So am I.' But not for hot ham and Parmesan-coated chicken. She backed onto the dance floor, drawing Jack with her. Her hands met behind his neck, her tummy pressed into him and her feet began moving in time with the music, quiet dinner music that most people were ignoring while they ate the meal. Jack's warm, hard body was all she needed right now. Jack was all she wanted to devour. He was the main course and the dessert.

His hands settled on her waist, drew her even closer to him. 'Ahh, Red. Some things just don't change, do they?' His lips kissed her forehead.

'But they do get better,' she whispered back, wondering how she would last the next few hours here without dragging Jack outside and into the back seat of his car. Talk about acting like a teenager. But that was how he made her feel, all hot anticipation and excitement. Her body tingled as his lips trailed kisses down her cheek.

The music stopped. Ruby tripped over her own shoes when Jack stopped too. His arms steadied her. 'Easy. How do you manage to stay on those stilts?'

'Stilts?' She leaned back in his arms and glared up into his laughing eyes. 'That's so not sexy.'

'Exactly. I'm trying to defuse the situation so we can get through the remainder of the evening.' He leaned closer. 'But they are the sexiest shoes I've ever seen.'

Her mouth dried. She managed to stutter, 'Th-that's better.' For a moment there she'd thought she'd been losing her touch when it came to teasing Jack.

'Ruby, come on, we've got to join the others for the speeches. It won't look good if the base manager is missing.'

'I hate it when you get all practical and proper.' But she took his hand and walked back to their table, struggling not to limp and wondering how late they had to stay. They didn't see the ball out.

They couldn't take the strain of dancing together so close they were as one, without wanting to get even closer. Jack drove fast, straight to Ruby's house. It was nearer than his. If he didn't get there in a very short minute he'd implode with needing her. Dancing with her had wound him tighter than a coiled spring. Hours of holding her body against his had raised his desire to impossible levels. Absorbing her scent had nearly tipped him over the edge—very publicly.

He braked sharply at Ruby's gate. Waving the automatic-locking device at his car, he raced up her path with her hand wrapped in his. If the car hadn't locked, too bad.

Ruby had her front door open faster than a burglar. They tore down the hall to her bedroom, not stopping for kisses on the way. They were way past needing to hold each other, or to kiss and take their time allowing the passion to build.

The passion was there, barely in control, sizzling along his veins. Jack tossed his jacket, tugged his shirt out, up and off. Caught Ruby to him as she reached the bed and felt behind for her zipper. 'Let me,' he murmured against her neck.

She swivelled around under his hands. 'Hurry.' And she shimmied out of her dress, her butt touching, teasing him.

Jack pulled her back against his chest; his hands found and kneaded her breasts. She arched them into him while her backside touched his manhood, pushed closer. Teasing, taunting, making him ache for her. Her hot hand slid between them, found him, rubbed him.

He wanted her, wanted to be inside her. Now. His hand slid downwards, caressing that silky skin from breast to navel, over her belly to the mound above her core, under her panties and into the warm, wet centre of the woman he loved. 'Ahh, Ruby,' he whispered against her neck, tasting her, spreading kisses over her hot skin.

Under his hand she moved, rocked onto her toes, rolled forward, back, forward, back. Between their bodies she continued to rub him. Jack gritted his teeth, attempting to hold back the desire roaring through him and threatening to spill out into her hand.

He'd waited a long time for this. He'd wanted

Red from the instant he'd set eyes on her again a few months ago. A few more minutes were nothing. He couldn't fall off the edge without taking Ruby with him. They were finally together again. They would finish this night wound around each other, their bodies blended into one.

Bracing himself, pulling her hand away, he concentrated on Ruby and only Ruby. Her moans of pleasure curled around him, and he turned her so he could taste her sweet mouth. 'I've missed you so much,' he groaned against her lips.

She kissed him back as though this was for the first time, for the millionth time. Fiercely, greedily. Tenderly, sweetly. All rolled into one life-changing kiss. Her breasts pressed against his chest, her hands clasped behind his neck, she tugged him backwards.

Jack backed her onto the bed and dropped down beside her, covered her body with his and slowly slid inside. Slowly slid home. Home where he belonged, had belonged all along.

Ruby put the phone down, marvelling that Jack hadn't been woken when Chris rang. Unless he was lying in bed, waiting for her to return for some more serious lovemaking. A warm glow settled over her. Last night it had been as though they'd never been apart, like they loved each other as much as ever. More than ever. Hands on hips, she stretched, arching her back, easing all her sweetly aching muscles.

She hopped over to the sideboard, saving her bad knee, and tugged open the drawer containing an assortment of bills, letters and brochures. She scrabbled through them until she found what Chris had asked for and tossed it over to the table, then turned to the fridge. If Jack wanted her back in bed he'd just have to wait while she cooked up a storm of bacon, eggs and hash browns. He'd always had a big appetite after the night before.

While the bacon sizzled gently she found a tray big enough to carry their breakfasts back to bed. A bubble of happiness grew inside her, pressing on her lungs, squashing her tummy, widening her smile. Her feet tap-danced a circle, her hands punched the air. Yee-ha.

Crack, two eggs in the pan. Suddenly Ruby's smile slipped. What if Jack wanted nothing other than the bed stuff? What if he didn't come home after his southern sojourn? Take it one day, one hour at a time. Jack was asleep in her bed after a hot night making love. She'd make the most of the moment and worry about the rest later.

Waiting for the eggs to cook, she eased her bad leg out straight. Sucked air through her teeth as her knee protested. All that dancing had turned it into a hot, throbbing glob in the middle of her leg. Shards of pain stabbed outward, up and down, slicing at her calf muscle, at her thigh. 'My own fault for doing the whoopee dance.'

Reaching up to a high shelf above the microwave, her fingers closed around a small bottle. Two painkillers would lighten the pain for a while. At least until Jack had left. The last thing she needed was for him to start nagging her about seeing a doctor. She already knew what her specialist would say, and she wasn't ready. A knee transplant would mean time off work, would probably mean the end of her career on the helicopters.

As she swallowed the tablets the injustice of everything began roiling in her stomach. Did reality mean she had to give up the job she loved? Was any job worth wrecking her body for? Her happiness slowly deflated.

She plonked down on a chair at the table and dropped her head in her hands. 'I'm not going there yet. I can't. Not after all the effort I've put in so I can have the right house, the perfect job. I'll have to take more care, not get so carried away. There's too much at stake.' Her happiness and heart.

'Trying too hard to convince yourself to stay, Ruby?'

Her head jerked up. Her eyes clashed with Jack's glinting ones as he leaned against the doorframe. 'I don't need convincing to stay in Wellington.'

'Sounds to me much like last time. Just as things are going very well you want to take a hike.' His face tightened, his lips pressed together. 'Just when I'd begun believing in you.'

'I'm still here, aren't I?' Slam bang went her heart against her ribs.

'For how long, Ruby? A week? A day? An hour?' His face was white. 'Save us a load of bother and go pack your bag.'

'You're quick to judge. Doesn't the night we've just shared mean anything to you? Or was I a way of easing your frustration?' She had thrown herself at him, but she'd believed they were on the same page.

His eyes narrowed as his gaze slid over her. 'How do you explain that little conversation I overheard you having with yourself? If that wasn't about leaving then I'm damned if I know what it was.'

Ruby slapped her hand on the tabletop, and let her temper get the better of her. 'My knee is giving me grief big time. The time is rapidly approaching when I have to have replacement surgery. And I'm not ready. I'll never be ready. I don't want to give up my work. I don't want to give up any of the things I'm trying to achieve here.'

His gaze dropped to under the table but he didn't say anything.

Goaded by his silence, she cried out at him, 'You don't want to understand. You don't care. You enjoyed last night, all of it, and don't even begin to deny that.' She stabbed the air between them. 'But already, almost before you've woken up, all you want to do is protect yourself from me. Fine, get out of here. I'll change crews for the rest of your time on the base. I don't need you in my life, Jack Forbes.'

He flinched, straightened and began to turn away. Stopped, turned back, his eyes widening as he stared at the table. Two long strides and he stood beside her, his hand snatching up the brochure she'd got out minutes ago. He flicked through it, his cheeks blanching.

Ruby stuttered, 'I—I can explain.'

'I bet you can. But I don't want your lies.' He slapped the brochure down. 'Why is it so hard for you to come out and say it? When were you going to tell me you're planning to move to Australia?' His finger stabbed the advertisement for staff at the flying doctors' base circled with blue ink. 'Is everything still about you? Your job. Your house. It used to be your father.'

'You're wrong.' She wasn't going to beg him to hear her out.

'How does it make you feel when you let people go from your life?' He played dirty.

'I came back because of you, Jack.' The instant disbelief in his eyes stabbed her through the heart. 'I do love my house and I'm proud of what I'm achieving with it but it's only a house. Same goes for my job. I'd leave it all for you.'

His eyes rolled towards the ceiling. 'And Zane? You going to dump him too?'

'He goes with me. Where are we going?' Her heart had stopped. He really didn't want to be a part of her life. His harsh goading hurt.

'You're going to Queensland. I'm going south.'

That was low. Anger stirred again, kick-started her heart. 'I don't owe you an explanation. You wanted honesty. How about trust? If you can't give me that then we have nothing.'

'Too right.' And he was gone, the back door slamming behind him.

Ruby folded her arms on the table and sank her head onto them. And gave in to the tears she'd never thought she'd have to cry over Jack again. The only man she'd loved. The man she still loved, stronger than ever. There'd be no more chances. She'd used up her last one.

Ruby crawled into her bed, concentrating on the throbbing in her knee in a vain attempt to ignore the agony in her heart. Stretching her legs out carefully, she rolled into the space where Jack had slept the last hour of last night. Pulling the covers up tight around her neck, she curled onto her side, tucking the pillow he'd used against her tender breasts. Her whole body ached from their lovemaking. It should've been a delicious sensation but now it felt bitter-sweet.

Inhaling his scent, she gave in to another wave of tears. One night with Jack and she'd been in heaven. He'd made love with a skill that had taken her breath away. Often. Very often. He'd given so freely, as if it was the only way he knew to share himself.

A doggy nose pressed against her back. Slowly she rolled over and came nose to nose with Zane. 'Hey, my boy. I still have you. It's back to you and me again.' If it had ever really been any different.

Zane plopped his head on the side of the bed and gazed at her adoringly. His head felt silky under her shaking hand. His eyes were full of love and trust. So much trust, so easily won with affection and food and warm shelter.

'Why can't he be like you?' *Hey, wake up, Ruby, smell the air. Your dream of getting back together is over before it even left the ground.*

Jack's heading out of town, without you. He won't be looking back.

Exactly as she'd done. Except she had looked back. Often. And finally she'd returned.

Sitting upright, she yanked at the covers as they threatened to slip off her. Red haze filled her head, coloured her sight.

Jack had no right to do this to her. He couldn't treat her so badly and expect to get away with it. No way. Who did he think he was to make love to her all night and then walk out on her? Not when he knew first hand how that felt.

She wasn't going to give up without a fight after all. If she won him back, anything she did now would be worth it. Urgency gripped her. She had to find him, make him talk to her, listen to her. They belonged together.

Tearing down the hall, she veered into the bathroom where she turned the shower on to heat up while she cleaned her teeth. She'd take an hour to prepare herself and to calm down or she might do more damage to their strained relationship when she saw him. Because they did have a relationship, one with good history. Jack was perfect for her. She was right for him. Hadn't he told her how she'd saved him that night years ago?

'I'll use my mallet on his head to make him see sense if I have to.'

She ducked into the shower box. 'Ahhhhhhhh!' She leapt straight back out. Grabbed a towel to wrap around her. Her teeth chattered, and goose-bumps covered her skin. The water was freezing.

Turning the shower off, she tried the hot water in the basin. Cold. Out in the kitchen the same result and the old hot-water cylinder was definitely on. The fuse hadn't popped on the meter board. The lights came on when she flicked switches so there was still power.

'Another disaster, but this one I'm going to suck up. I can deal with it. Easily.' She gave herself a quick, cold sluice before pulling on a thick jersey and tight-fitting jeans. She shoved her feet into thick woollen socks and tied on her boots. Then she rang the plumber.

'I've got a bit of a problem.' By the time she hung up her head was hurting. Hot-water cylinders didn't come cheap. Of course they wouldn't. That would've been working in her favour and so far today showed no signs of being at all friendly. *Be tough, be strong.*

She debated for two seconds about walking around to Jack's house. 'Sorry, Zane, you'll have to wait for your walk. I'm taking the truck.' The truck would be quicker. And it gave a boost to her confidence to be seen behind the steering-wheel, made her feel a few sizes taller. And she was going to need all the confidence and good luck and patience she could muster when she came face to face with Jack. She had to get this right or she'd spend the rest of her life debating with herself how she could've done it differently to keep Jack.

She'd have charged inside without knocking if his front door hadn't been locked. Instead she leaned on the bell until she heard the door being unlocked.

'Jack, what do you think you're...?' She spluttered to a stop, staring at the man standing in front of her, his eyes chilly, his face blank. 'Steve.'

'Ruby.' Jack's brother made no move to let her enter.

'I didn't know you were home.'

'Why would you?'

Jack might have mentioned it last night when they were still getting on. She shrugged away her disappointment. Same old Jack, not talking about anything going on in his life. 'Can I come in? I need to see Jack.'

'He's not here. He won't be back until late to-morrow night.' Was that a flicker of sympathy in his face? Not likely. Steve had never been her friend.

'Are you sure he's not here?' Steve would be loving her desperation. He'd done his best to come between her and Jack three years ago and he'd never hidden his delight when he'd learned she was leaving.

'Jack left half an hour ago for Auckland.' Steve held the door wide. 'Want a coffee? I've just made a pot.'

Her eyes popped. What? Steve inviting her in? To prove Jack really wasn't here? Or to be friendly? Either way, she wasn't staying. 'No, thanks. I just needed to see Jack, explain some-thing to him, but it'll have to wait until work on Tuesday.'

She turned for the stairs and her truck. How

would she get through the weekend? Go to Auckland? Definitely not.

'Ruby,' Steve called. 'Wait.'

'What ever for?' That red haze was returning. These brothers stuck together no matter what, never giving an outsider a chance.

'Give Jack a break. Hear him out when he gets back home. Please.' Steve was pleading with her?

'Hear him out? Getting him to talk in the first place would be a start.'

'He gave you a chance three years ago, Ruby. He worked hard at seeing things your way, broke his heart over you because he knew it was right to let you go. Please.'

'Please' twice in one conversation, in one life-time. Her mouth dropped, the haze retreated. Steve wanted her to give Jack a chance? Steve was helping her with Jack? What was this about? 'About that coffee?'

She followed Steve through to the kitchen and perched on a barstool, watching him fill a plunger with grinds and boiling water. 'How long are you back for?'

'A week. My next leave happens when Jack's

gone to Scott Base so I figured I'd come home now.'

'I'm still struggling to believe he's going there. It's so not Jack.' She got off the stool, wandered across to the bay window and gazed out at the harbour way below.

'Who knows? It could be the best thing for him. Dad and I kept him tied here, looking out for us, for too long. It's time for him to sort out what he wants to do for himself.' Steve lifted his head, his eyes connecting with hers. 'I'll rephrase that. Jack needs to admit to what he already knows he wants and go after it.'

'And what would that be?' Obviously not her.

'You'll have to ask him.' Steve pushed a full mug in her direction.

When she sipped the hot liquid her eyebrows rose. 'You want to teach Jack how to make coffee this good before you go away again?'

'That sounds like you intend coming around here some more.' Steve leaned his elbows on the bar.

'That's up to your brother.' If he opened up to her after she explained about the brochure. After she told him how much she loved him.

'You two need your heads knocked together. Hard.' Steve's mug banged on the bench. 'Whatever happened to sitting down and talking things out like normal adults?'

Ruby squirmed on her stool. Steve wasn't just mad at her, he included his brother in the equation. 'You want me to sort things out with Jack? Once and for all?'

He rolled his eyes heavenward. 'At last, the woman gets it.'

CHAPTER TWELVE

'ARE you stopping over in Auckland tonight, Dr Forbes?' The flight attendant hovered over Jack, her breasts pushed almost into his face.

'Yes, I am.'

'Alone?'

'No.' *Now leave me alone. Go pick on some other bloke.*

Jack watched her slink down the aisle, relieved she'd got the message, guilty for being so abrupt. But he wasn't in the mood for idle chit-chat. He was angry. At Red? Who else? He swallowed the hot lump in his throat, slumped further down in his seat. No, not at Red, at himself.

He was an idiot. Too busy protecting his heart to think about the hurt he'd inflict by walking out on her. After snarling cutting criticism that had sliced into her. Oh, yeah, he'd seen the instant the pain had struck.

But what else could he do? Admit how much

he needed her? How her strength was his pillar? That would terrify her. A sure way to get her packing up again.

Be honest, Jacko. Red isn't leaving. You're the one running away and it feels bad. Feels totally, totally wrong. How had Ruby done it so often?

Different scenario, Jacko. She was searching for her father, not running away.

He tried stretching his legs in the cramped space under the seat in front of him. Gave up. Airplanes weren't designed for anyone taller than—than Ruby. Leaning his head back, he closed his eyes and immediately saw Red. She was dancing by, laughing, teasing, waving at him in that black dress. He blinked. Red didn't disappear. Now her face had crumpled with sadness, but that chin was still jutting out in defiance. Gutsy. Strong. Lovable.

She'd said she'd go anywhere with him, give up her job and house for him. And he'd stomped on her words. Did she give second chances? He'd have to dig deep, open himself up to her in a way he'd never done in his life. It'd be excruciating. It would be worth it if she listened.

'Ladies and gentlemen, shortly we'll be landing in Auckland.'

Jack popped his eyes open. Auckland. Dad. Family.

What about Wellington? Ruby. Family. And a house, a wacky dog and maybe a job in February.

At the airline counter Jack was gutted when told he'd have to wait till the next day to return to Wellington. 'Are you saying all the flights are full?'

The assistant shook her head in disbelief. 'You've just landed and you have to ask why there are no flights?' He must have looked stunned because she added, 'They're about to close the airport. Wellington shut half an hour ago. Didn't you find your flight very bumpy?'

He'd had more important things on his mind.

By Monday afternoon Ruby was so tense she thought she'd go crazy if she didn't see Jack soon. But despite the zillion texts she'd sent, he hadn't answered.

She spun the truck's steering-wheel and parked outside her gate. Letting her head drop back against the seat, she grimaced. At least she'd sorted some things out in town, had begun the processes for major changes. Changes she'd never thought she'd make and now that she'd instigated them she felt surprisingly light-hearted about them.

Her cellphone chattered. Grabbing it, she read the name flashing back at her. Not Jack. Tossing the phone into her bag, she picked up her grocery bags and eased down to the road carefully, favouring her knee.

Zane barked as she pushed open the gate and rubbed his ears. 'Hey, boy. Did you miss me?'

Thump. Thump. Thump.

'What's that?' Straightening up, Ruby followed the heavy sounds to the corner of her house where she stopped abruptly. Leaned against the wall for support. And ogled the view.

Jack, shirt off, swung an axe at the stump of her old walnut tree. Swing, slam. Swing, slam. My, oh, my. The man had some muscles. They rippled down his back. They flexed in his arms. They held his stomach taut. Her mouth dried, her tongue did circuits. He'd felt good, strong and hard, during their lovemaking on Saturday night, but now? Now she had to restrain herself from rushing over and running her hands all over that sweat-coated body.

Flip-flop went her heart, like a tadpole out of water. Heck, she could go on watching him for ever, drinking in the sight.

Zane had other ideas. He picked up his ball and trotted over to Jack, nudged his thigh. Jack slammed the axe into a root and turned to pat Zane. That was when he saw her. His gaze clashed with hers. His face filled with uncertainty. 'Red, I hope it's okay to start on removing this stump.'

She blindly placed her bags on the porch and advanced slowly towards Jack. Her heart started an erratic beat. 'It has to come out some time and I can't get a bulldozer out here to haul it from the ground.'

'That's what I thought.' His eyes still held hers.

'You have nothing better to do with your afternoon?'

He swallowed. Nodded. 'Yeah, I did. But you weren't here.'

'You knew I wouldn't have gone far, right?'

'Zane told me.' He looked away, looked back. 'Yeah, I knew. I don't know what that brochure was about but I already figured you wouldn't lie to me. You never have. I got it horribly wrong so I figured I'd got other things wrong too.'

'To clear up one thing, the brochure belongs to Chris. He's got a surprise trip organised for Sandra. He couldn't leave them in his locker at work because she's in and out of it as often as her own.'

Jack crossed the lawn to stand in front of her. 'I'm not very good at talking about me.'

His blunt statement took her breath away. 'It's okay.'

'No, it's not. I hated it when you left to go to the States. I wanted to ask you to stay a few more months so we could go together. But that would've meant telling you how afraid of being left behind I was and why. I couldn't do that. To tell you that everyone left me at some time in my life would've made me look like a loser, like the kind of man no one wanted around for ever.'

'Jack, no. Don't ever think that. People don't leave you. They go out into the world on their own journeys, strong from your love and knowing you'll always be there for them.' Ruby reached for his hands, held them tightly. 'They're not running away from you. They haven't stopped loving you. I never stopped loving you. Not for one second.'

'So why didn't you come look me up when you got back?'

She grinned, a slightly strained grin but one nevertheless. 'The blonde sticking plaster.'

'What?' He stared at her as though she'd grown a third eye.

Ruby quickly explained, and Jack relaxed, pulled her close and wrapped his arms around her. 'You're my only love, ruby-red girl. Always have been.' They stood in the spring sun, holding each other until Zane nudged them.

Ruby wiped her eyes. Somehow they'd become damp. 'You weren't the only one at fault. I should've talked to you before I went away. I wanted to wait for you but didn't think you'd agree to go with me.'

'I think now that I would've.' Jack kissed the tip of her nose.

'At the time I was so antsy. And the Greaser was my battle. I don't think I wanted to share him.' She kissed Jack's mouth. There'd been a lot of things she hadn't shared. From now on she'd tell Jack everything. So, 'I've been to see the base doctor today. My knee has been getting worse. A few bad landings, a lot of dancing. I've made a decision.' She sucked air, again surprised that this didn't hurt much. 'I'm quitting the helicopters and going to work on the ambulances. There's a job coming up in the city next month.'

His face registered surprise. 'I knew you were having trouble but I thought you'd keep on jumping out of helicopters for a long time to come.'

She shook her head. 'I want to dance with you again. Often. I want to be able to run on the beach with my kids. Knee replacements are all very well but let's not go there any sooner than necessary.'

His mouth covered hers. A deep, lingering kiss, only to be interrupted by Zane again. Jack laughed and took Ruby's hand, turning her round. 'Look, there in the corner by your vegetable patch.'

'A new walnut tree. Awesome.' Ruby stared at the tree, a giggle rolling up her throat, breaking free. 'With two toy plastic swings hanging on the branch.' She swivelled around to Jack. 'A pink one and a blue one. Jack, what are you planning?'

He counted on his fingers. 'Making you my wife. Having a baby with my wife. Having another baby with my wife. Starting back in A and E in February after I've been on my honeymoon with my wife.' His smile was so male, so self-satisfied. 'I'm still going south so I thought…' he glanced at her '…hoped we could get married as soon as I get back.'

Ruby threw herself into his arms and started a thorough kissing campaign.

Zane finally gave up trying to get their attention and went to study the contents of Ruby's grocery bags. When the humans finally came up for air the dog had devoured the steak Ruby had planned on having for dinner.

Ruby laughed out loud. 'Naughty boy.' She patted his head. 'Now I'll have to cook something else. You like lasagne, Jack?'

'Why don't I take you out somewhere? We can leave the heat-and-eat stuff for another less important day.' He wisely stepped back, out of arm's range.

Ruby wagged her finger at him as she approached. 'I'll tell you this for nothing, Mr Smarty Pants. I've been taking cooking lessons and I can rustle up a fine meal any time I like now.' She sprang at Jack, catching him as he tried to dodge sideways.

They went down in a heap on the lawn. As Jack wound his arms around Red again he grinned. 'Now I know this day is a total dream. I'm going to wake up and find two-minute noodles on the table and you standing over me with a whip until I eat them.'

'Do I get to wear black stockings and a lacy body suit?' Ruby covered his oath with her mouth and kissed him senseless.

* * * * *

Mills & Boon® Large Print

Medical

December

January

February

Mills & Boon® Large Print Medical

March

HER MOTHERHOOD WISH	Anne Fraser
A BOND BETWEEN STRANGERS	Scarlet Wilson
ONCE A PLAYBOY…	Kate Hardy
CHALLENGING THE NURSE'S RULES	Janice Lynn
THE SHEIKH AND THE SURROGATE MUM	Meredith Webber
TAMED BY HER BROODING BOSS	Joanna Neil

April

A SOCIALITE'S CHRISTMAS WISH	Lucy Clark
REDEEMING DR RICCARDI	Leah Martyn
THE FAMILY WHO MADE HIM WHOLE	Jennifer Taylor
THE DOCTOR MEETS HER MATCH	Annie Claydon
THE DOCTOR'S LOST-AND-FOUND HEART	Dianne Drake
THE MAN WHO WOULDN'T MARRY	Tina Beckett

May

MAYBE THIS CHRISTMAS…?	Alison Roberts
A DOCTOR, A FLING & A WEDDING RING	Fiona McArthur
DR CHANDLER'S SLEEPING BEAUTY	Melanie Milburne
HER CHRISTMAS EVE DIAMOND	Scarlet Wilson
NEWBORN BABY FOR CHRISTMAS	Fiona Lowe
THE WAR HERO'S LOCKED-AWAY HEART	Louisa George

NEATH PORT TALBOT LIBRARY
AND INFORMATION SERVICES

217	25		49	71/3	73	
	26		50		74	
	27		51		75	
			52		7	